Born in the Grave Part 2

Self Made Tay

Lock Down Publications and Ca$h
Presents
BORN IN THE GRAVE 2
A Novel by *Self Made Tay*

Self Made Tay

Lock Down Publications
Po Box 944
Stockbridge, Ga 30281

Visit our website @
www.lockdownpublications.com

Lock Down Publications
Like our page on Facebook: Lock Down Publications @
www.facebook.com/lockdownpublications.ldp
Book interior design by: **Shawn Walker**
Edited by: **Nuel Uyi**

Stay Connected with Us!

Text **LOCKDOWN** to 22828 to stay up-to-date with new releases, sneak peaks, contests and more…
Thank you.

Submission Guideline.

Submit the first three chapters of your completed manuscript to ldpsubmissions@gmail.com, subject line: Your book's title. The manuscript must be in a .doc file and sent as an attachment. Document should be in Times New Roman, double spaced and in size 12 font. Also, provide your synopsis and full contact information. If sending multiple submissions, they must each be in a separate email.

Have a story but no way to send it electronically? You can still submit to LDP/Ca$h Presents. Send in the first three chapters, written or typed, of your completed manuscript to:

LDP: Submissions Dept
Po Box 944
Stockbridge, Ga 30281

DO NOT send original manuscript. Must be a duplicate.

Provide your synopsis and a cover letter containing your full contact information.

Thanks for considering LDP and Ca$h Presents.

ACKNOWLEDGEMENTS

Big shout out to Cash and LockDown Publications. I can't express how grateful I am in one lifetime. Together, I pray we prosper and grow in strength. So much thanks for the chance you guys have given me. I thank God for blessing you and I appreciate you sharing your blessing. All praise is due to Allah.

Chapter 1 Flex's Justification
Scene: The Murder scene

This dumb-ass nigga is always getting into shit. Then, expect me to clean shit up. Look at these dumb ass pigs. They are so thirsty for an arrest; they would cuff anything overlooking the real predators. Lucky me, I guess.

Oh, my bad, my name is Flex by the way. You probably remember me. I heard my brother tried to brainwash you with a whole bunch of bullshit. Fuck with me. I'm gonna give you the real me. Besides, after this, I don't think the dude is gone be able to talk anymore.

Let me backtrack a couple of moments so you won't be lost. I was supposed to meet my brother Q on the one way. That's where I had intended to only rob him and send him on his way. On my way, my eyes caught the chance of a two-for-one deal, or should I say three? Two police officers by the street names of Tall and Short were searching the trunk of Q's car, looking. I thought it was real stupid of them to be slipping at a time like this. The residents of Richmond City were literally at war with the RPD. About a few weeks ago, there was a bloodbath just on the next street over on Saint John. If you want to know the details, you should have checked in with Q. I ain't got time to go back that far. Right now, I had to focus on these kills.

Bow! I dropped Tall first. He was somewhat of the biggest threat. I looked towards Q's dumb ass standing there in handcuffs with a smile on his face. What the fuck, he thought he was on? An Avenger movie? I ain't come to save that nigga. I'm doing this shit for the hood.

As expected, Short attempted to draw his weapon. I ain't give him a chance. Bow! Bow! I placed two in his head from the Glock .40. A part of me wanted to snatch my mask off so that dick-sucking ass oppressor could see the angel of death yanking his soul out of his throat. If I had done that, it would have made me just as dumb as these three dick heads. For now, I could live with self-satisfaction. Tall and Short have been harassing niggas ever since I could remember. This moment was a dream come true.

I never in a million years imagined that it would come down to this with Q and me. For a fact, I knew that he knew it was me. The fact that I didn't know, was if I could trust him beyond this point. Dude done got on some change of heart type shit. He was trying to pack up and leave with everything we built. I can't have that. I felt like Bleek on Coming of Age. Therefore, I felt forced to throw him a birthday party.

I swung the .40 in his direction, for someone who always seems to foresee shit, he sure did look surprised. I ain't gone lie; I haven't had a conscience when it came to murder since my first kill. For some reason, this felt like the very first one again. I could have been tripping, but it felt like the gun was becoming heavier in my hand. Using the thoughts of all the money and power that I wanted from Q, I dropped my nuts and raised the pistol to a higher level. Q tried to duck but it was way too late. A bullet caught him in the head. The dead weight from his body collapsed to the ground. Landing him in an awkward position with his hand cuffed behind his back. All Q ever wanted was to be free. It's fucked up that he had to die in bondage by the hands of his own blood, but fuck him, I gotta get the fuck out of here.

I stepped over the corpse of my father's son. "Tell Pops I said wat up when you get up der fo' me fool," I uttered under my breath. I opened the driver's car door and immediately spotted the keys lying on the seat. This shit was too easy. Well, at least, so I thought until I looked through the rearview mirror. I was so anxious to get away that I almost forgot to close the trunk. After I hopped out and did so, I was gone.

That nigga Q had the plug, the money; somehow, he snatched up the hood, and was well on his way to running the city. He did most of that off my muscles. It was my idea to take over the One Way. After we did that, it was me who put that shit together. I'm the one that gave Q a spot around Creighton Court Projects, allowing him to expand his clientele. Now when shit got real and started to bounce back off the fan, he was ready to say fuck all of us that risked it all for him. Fuck that, it's a new King in town. You can't leave your throne unguarded and still think you are gone wear the crown. That nigga wasn't a real King anyway. How the fuck do you have all that power and still working on a construction site? Where the fuck do they do that? The dude was faking, but I'm a …… Hold up right quick fool. This is that clown-ass nigga Hawk ringing my line. Let me see what the dude wants and Ima get back to you.

"Hello!"

Self Made Tay

Chapter 2: The Death of Q
Scene: The murder scene

I'm telling you; it pays to have a nigga like Flex on your team. There's nothing like having a hitter on your team that's willing to kill for you for free, no matter what. This nigga was creeping up behind two blue suits right now as I speak.

I watched as Flex upped the Glock popping the top of Tall's noggin. His head burst open like a watermelon crashing to the ground from three stories up. I couldn't help but smile. All my anxieties had just been released and were floating away like a butterfly fresh out of the cocoon.

Short tried to reach for his hip, Flex already had his gun pointed at a headshot angle. He spared him for a quick second allowing Short to think that he actually had a chance. That second was over fast. In the next second to come, two bullets were released from Flex's gun. It seemed like it took Short's body forever to tumble.

Don't judge me, but at that moment, I thanked God for this demon that he sent from up above. Sometimes your blessings may come in a disastrous fashion. I stood tall waiting to be released from the cuffs by my brother.

I always tried to plan a few steps ahead. However, these past few moments had me in a heap of mixed emotions clouding my judgments and blinding my vision. Things were beginning to seem impractical. A nigga life then goes so crazy that you could script that bitch and make a movie out of it. And, if you do, I want my percentage.

Just when I thought shit couldn't get any more unpredictable, Flex aimed the gun in my direction. It must have been somebody behind me or something, at least that's what I wanted to believe. However, the look in Flex's eyes spoke volumes. For reasons unknown to my knowledge, I was definitely his intended target.

Being the interpreter that I was, I anticipated for Flex to take one shot to my head. I knew he liked to aim high as well, so I

13

dropped my body to the ground in a ducking motion. The firearm exploded. My heart dropped. The bullet pierced the upper part of my head. I could barely feel my body slamming to the ground. My sight was doubled as if my eyes had a vision of their own. My outside light was beginning to darken as my eyelids flickered. A light that was brighter than I have ever witnessed was illuminated from within. I felt departed from myself. Felt like I could fly, but my body remained stiff, glued to the pavement. I started to feel light and cold, like a ghost, and then, I felt nothing.

I found myself surrounded by a great silence. Darkness in every direction I attempted to look. I had reached an unknown plane. There was no way I could plan my way out of this.

Chapter 3: Keyshia's Worst Nightmare
Scene: Her Home

Bow! Bow! Bow! Bow!

"Mommy! Dey shooting again," my second oldest daughter screamed out. I swear that little girl was too grown. I was embarrassed to say honestly, but she and her sister were used to the sound of gunfire.

"Girl, take your ass upstairs to yo room Mia," I ordered her. Usually, I wouldn't pay this type of shit any mind, but my intuition was alarming me of my sweet nightmares. I know that the only reason why I was so concerned was that my daughter's father had just left out that back door only a matter of minutes ago.

"Lord, let me go make sure this ain't his ass dis time," I uttered to myself, sliding on my slippers. Q was always in some dumb shit. The crazy part about it was that it was never for the wrong he did. Shit, the only person he seemed to do wrong to was me. Q had a good heart that always landed him in bad situations. He is always trying to give people shit that they ain't want. Like love, peace, unity, and all that positive shit. I have been trying to tell his ass that if it ain't money or drugs, then these people out Jackson Ward don't want shit to do with his ass. Oh yeah, don't forget about them thirsty ass hoes. They would suck dick for a pill out this bitch.

I exited through the back door and proceeded along the same path that I assumed that Q had taken. Of course, over a hundred prying eyes were already out speculating. I could feel death flowing through the air. You could damn near smell it. Must be somebody important because it was more than a handful of people crying. As I strolled by, an older lady stared at me with saddened eyes. I wanted to ask her what the fuck she was looking at me like that for, but I realized something that puzzled my thoughts.

This was the first time I've ever seen caution tape wrapped around a police car. Usually, the cars were on the other side of the tape. Like the rest of the cars out here were. As I got closer, my heart dropped to my gut. I could no longer feel it beating. This shit was like déjà vu. A scene snatched straight out of the same nightmares that kept me up for the past two months. This shit couldn't be real.

Right before my eyes, Q's body was crumbled up in the middle of the street. If I didn't notice at first, I could feel it now. All eyes were on me. Without even knowing, I fell to my knees. Immediately, my eyes were filled with tears. I screamed at the top of my lungs. A scream that was deaf to my own ears.

People were approaching me trying to embrace me in comfort. I didn't want anybody to touch me. All I wanted at the point was for someone to touch the mother fucker that did this shit to my baby's daddy. "Get da fuck out from round me," I yelled. "All ya'll." They formed a circle-like shape around me. "Why God!? Why!?"

As best as I could, I stood to my feet, rushing the crowd swinging with vengeance. "Who da fuck did dis to him?" My blows flew through the wind. "I know one of yall bitches know some," I said to no one in particular.

Out of nowhere, a pair of arms were wrapped around my torso. The embrace was strong and held me tight. I tried to wiggle out of the grip, but it was a struggle that I couldn't win. "Calm down sis. I got you." A voice spoke to my ear.

"Who da fuck is dis?" I really wanted to know. Then again, I didn't care who it was. I wanted to be freed. "Get da fuck off me!" I demanded. "It's Burga Keyshia, and I ain't lettin' you go til you calm down."

I really wasn't trying to hear that shit. Still, though, I calmed down a bit. Well, at least I acted like I did. As Burga was slowly unleashing his grip on me, the paramedics were lifting Q up on a stretcher. I went into a crazed rage again. "Why da fuck do ya'll still have da fucking handcuffs on him fo?" I questioned. A few bystanders gathered with me in protest. Instead of taking the handcuffs off, they pulled the sheet over his face and rolled him through the doors of the ambulance. I knew then that it was over. Everything was over. Felt like my whole life was over. Why couldn't he have just listened to me? I tried to warn him. I practically begged him to leave these wicked ass streets alone. After everything that he has done for these streets, this is how they repay him? I was frozen from my brain to my heart, down to my toes. The only thing moving on me was the tears that ran down my face. Drowning me in my own sorrows.

Now, Reggie was walking up. He stopped in front of me, wrapped his arms around me and laid my head on his shoulders. Reggie was one of Q's long-time close friends. Up to this point, I always felt like Q was safe in these streets as long as Reggie was around. After this though, I didn't trust a soul. "Ima handle dis shit sis. I promise."

There was no telling who was behind this shit. I know that no one is exempt from death. But Q was very calculated, cautious, and sometimes even nervous. He was also smarter than what people gave him credit for. His instincts were strong. He could sense danger from days away. I don't know who it was that did the hit. I just know that this had to have been a blind side tackle.

Self Made Tay

Chapter 4: Down's Regret
Scene" The Murder Scene

I felt Keyshia's pain. I wanted to snap out as bad as she did. A part of me felt like I didn't deserve to. I had already been selfish enough. Even though it wasn't intentional, I had snatched her man away from her emotionally. Now I had to stand by and witness her lose him wholly. To be honest, I lost a piece of my heart as well.

Q was something special. He was different. Sweet, but tough. He never told me that he loved me, but he always found ways to show it. I never once told him that I loved him, but now I'm wishing that I did.

My biggest regret was my latest one. I just had Q in my face, standing right in my living room. I was happy as I don't know when to see him, but my bipolar ways ran him away. I was chewing his head off about him being missing for so long. He had gone weeks without checking in with me. I wasn't used to that. I had become spoiled by the attention he showered me with. Also, I was worried to death for him. With all the things he was going through, I would have thought that he would have been got murdered. There was even a time when both of us could have been killed in an ambushed shootout. It hardened my heart to say this, but I kind of saw this coming. Even harder to admit was the fact that I really wanted him to stay with me instead of leaving. I really wanted to smile instead of crying, and I really wanted to fuck, instead of arguing.

Do you know what makes the situation even more fucked up? It's the fact that I'm pregnant with Q's baby right now. How do I explain this to my child?

After they carted his body off, I couldn't take it anymore. I couldn't stand that I had to stand by feeling invisible while Keyshia received all the attention. Was I jealous? Damn right, I was. At least she got to mourn with support. Whether she wanted it or not. I, on the other hand, was left to fend for myself once again. So, that's what I was going home to do. Be by myself.

Once I was secure in my home, I flopped down on the couch with my head down. Tears started to trickle down my cheeks. Beside me sat a Chanel bag. Q had just left it here probably twenty minutes ago. I guess it was a pardon gift. Even though Chanel was my favorite, I cursed his ass out. I was pissed because he had the nerve to bring me a bag when he knew we had a baby on the way. I picked the bag up and hugged it tightly. When I squeezed the bag, I realized how firm it was. This bag was far from empty. In fact, it was full. I opened the bag and was face to face with crispy blue hundred-dollar bills, clean fifties, and stacks of twenties. I cried uncontrollably. Once again, his actions spoke louder than his words.

Chapter 5: Flex's Frustrations
Scene: The One Way

I knew that car I had just taken from Q was evidence of a triple homicide and potential robbery that involved two police officers. For those same reasons, I parked that bitch in a spot behind the graveyard. It would be good there for at least a few hours, or until shit cooled off. Whichever one happened first.

I was on foot walking down Baker Street, the One Way. Headed to a block that we called The Carter-Ward. Yeah, I made that shit up myself. Q tried to take the credit on some 48 Laws of Power shit. My big brother's biggest flaw was that he always thought he was smarter than me. The whole time I was sitting in the cut playing him like a card until it was time to change the game up and go for the checkmate. I know you probably saying a nigga grimey, petty, larceny, wild or whatever, but I don't give a fuck. You don't even know me. You don't know my story. So, until you do, you don't judge me.

I'm pretty sure you know this by now, but Q and I were brothers through the same father. In proper terms, my mother was an addict. In real nigga words, Shawty was a straight crack head. I'm talking about a fiend all the way out. See, pops was a mixture of Q and I all in one. He was a certified hustler and a master murderer. He was a true country boy from South Boston or Halifax, Virginia. In the late '80s his siblings, a few cousins, and him migrated to the city of Richmond, Virginia. That's where he had us.

Pops was in love with Q's mother on some high school sweetheart type shit. She was born and raised in the projects of Jackson Ward. She was aspiring to become a doctor and well on her way. That was until I came along. Pops had a side relationship with my mother and had impregnated her. In exchange, my mother introduced my father to using the very same drugs that he sold. My Pops got strung out on my mother and together they got strung out on drugs.

Years went by as I got older. Through attention and attendance, I grew in my father's favor. Eventually, my father stuck with my mom. Every now and then, I knew that he would creep back with Q's mom. It took her a while, but before I knew it, she was seeing another dude. They fell for each other fast. I don't think Pops liked that. Long story short, Pops tried to slide through on the creep tip and ended up getting caught red-handed. I don't know how he was slipping that bad, but he was. Dude smoked my pops. Come to find out, Q's mother was still madly in love with Pops. She ended up killing her boyfriend for killing her baby daddy. With Q's mother behind bars, mine sucking on a glass dick, and our father dead and gone, all we had was each other. Well, I guess all I had now was me. Fuck it. I ain't tripping.

Ever since the hood found out that Q was dead, everybody has been blowing my phone up. That's all that nigga Hawk wanted earlier. To be the first person to tell me what he thought I didn't know. This time, it was Reggie calling. You ain't got to slide off. Just give me a minute to check his temperature.

"Yo," I answered.

"Lil brah," was all Reggie said.

"I already know brah," I replied, kind of sad for real.

"Niggas gotta do some homework brah. Somebody gotta pay fo' dis'."

"I'm already reading between da lines fool. When da time comes, niggas gone definitely teach a nigga a lesson. You hear me?"

"Yea, you know' I'm always in class on time. Front row seats. How you feelin' though fool? You fight?"

"I can't even say bra. I don't think dis shit is even processing yet. I can't believe dis shit is real."

"I feel you. Just keep yo' head up and if you ever need me, jus hit me up. Matter of fact, where are you?"

"One Way."

"Give me a minute. I'm ready. Pull up."

"Already." I hung up the phone and came up on the back of The Carter Ward. My first stop was a spot that we referred to as the Money House. Every room in this bitch used to be filled up with bands of every type of dollar. Shit got so real that I had to buy a money machine to help us count the money. Q was damn near star-struck when I first showed him. A moment of pride for me.

This shit was dry now. A damn near empty apartment, with a table, money machine and cooch. I flopped down on the couch and thought back to the days when business was booming. This shit went from the Money House to a personal duck-off spot. Now that the money was gone, so were the bodies that once flowed through this bitch. It was time to get this bitch back popping for good.

I drifted deep in thought about the money and drugs that I was almost certain Q had in the trunk. Greedy bastard, probably had well over a million dollars in the cut. Nigga ain't even think about leaving me shit. I had to give it to him though, dude had a mean grind. I don't know too many niggas personally that had a couple of steps up on the plug. He had an all-money-in mentally. He wasn't afraid to take risk for gain. Most of his gambles paid off nicely. With that being said, it wasn't a telling how many bricks that nigga had laid in the trunk. I was ready to put all that shit together. I just needed a plan. What would Q do?

My phone had started to ring again. I swear I was one call away from throwing this shit on the roof. It was nobody but my little nigga Wolf. The discussion won't even be worth repeating. He was just amped to ride on the person who had just killed my brother. It was kind of comical. I wondered what his reaction would be if I told him it was me. Anyway, he said he was in the kick back spot and wanted me to pull up.

I stashed the murder weapon in the money house and exchanged it for another dirty pistol. The difference was that one was a throw-away and the other was a souvenir. Next, I headed out the back door of the third-floor apartment and dropped down one level to the second where the kick-back spot was. As I was coming down the stairs, Reggie was coming up, meeting me on a second-floor level.

"Sup lil brah?" He asked me with puppy saddened eyes.

"Sup fool?" I was trying my best to clear up my dried emotions. With no words, Reggie's response was actual. He did something that was unusual for this cold-hearted killer. He wrapped his arms around me and hugged me. If you knew me, then you would know how much I hated fucking hugs. Still, though, I had to play my role. I slowly wrapped my arms around my longtime friend slash mentor.

"Dat's my word brah, we gone get whoever did this shit, even if it's da last thing I do," Reggie guaranteed me.

"Already brah." Was all I could muster. Once Reggie was off all that sentimental shit, I was free to enter the apartment. He followed me in. The kick-back spot was still the place to be. When Q had reigned, all drugs and guns were prohibited in this apartment, for criminal purposes, but since we've been killing police anyway, we all said fuck it.

Wolf was in the kitchen with a nigga named Spazz. They called him that because he did a lot of loud mouthing and never any action. They were playing the game as usual. Wolf saw me, dropped the PlayStation controller, and stood to his feet. Spazz remained seated.

Wolf was a few years younger than me, 20 years. The face full of facial hair made his features seem older than he actually was, resembling a wolf. He was short, slim but sinewy. "Sup big brah?" he asked. "Wat's da word?" "I ain't heard shit yet."

"Word on da street is dat shit was an inside job," Spazz spat out. Speaking out of turn. "You know Q been ghost fo' a minute now. Somebody had to know he was ready, pop out and had time to plan da hit in advance. Plus, dey say whoever did that, took da car cuz dey knew he had about 20 bricks in da trunk. Somebody back doored my nigga." He shook his head upon completing his statement.

"Where da fuck you hear all dis shit from?" Reggie asked. I got tired of hearing dis shit already. Knowing that most of the shit that Spazz said was accurate pissed me off even more. The only part that gave me hope was the sound of the twenty bricks.

"Leave that street gossip in da streets. Dis circle tight and we know who is who and who doing wat." I felt the need to express myself.

"I feel you Flex but think about it brah. When you put two and two together, shit jus doesn't add up. How da fuck ... on some cowboy shit straight out the wild west, I drew my pistol from my waist and sent a bullet from the gun to Spazz's hip. I raised the level of the pistol aiming at his head. Bow! Bow! With no hesitation, I dropped him.

Reggie looked puzzled. Wolf expressed a more aghast look. I was unbothered. I had just killed my only sibling; my father was dead and I'd probably put my mother out of her misery if I ever ran into her again. Killing Spazz was like stepping on a roach. I was already hot-headed, but from this point on, I felt for anyone who stood on my bad side.

"Wat da fuck you do that fo'?" Reggie wanted to know still looking confused.

"Ion," I replied. "Shidd dude talks too much. Fuck him. Dat nigga ain't gang anyway. I just wanna kill some fo' real brah. Dis shit gotta nigga frustrated.

"I thought I was crazy," Reggie confessed. "Let's get da fuck outta here."

Chapter 6: Q's Resurrection
Scene: Unknown

"Welcome Dequan," I heard a strange but oddly familiar voice greet me.

"Who is that?" I asked still unable to see anything, including a person.

"It's your ghost."

"My ghost?" I was sure I asked myself in my head.

"I can hear you," the voice enlightened me.

"Where am I?"

"The darkness."

"I thought I was dead?"

"Are you?" That had to be a trick question. Here I was so blinded that I couldn't even see myself. I had no feelings emotionally or physically. On top of that, I was talking to a voice whom I had no proof of its source. I definitely thought I was dead. Somehow, it seemed as if my thoughts lived on.

"Depending on what you claim death to be. That's the only way you may find our answer." The voice added. Whoever or whatever this person talking to me was, is an enigma to my understanding. The confusion was beginning to become aggravating. However, I had no actual feelings to experience the emotion. Yet, I understood them.

"Could you please tell me where I am? And what I'm doing here?" I asked with humility.

"Sure, I can," said the voice. "You are at the beginning of your existence. The origin of your creation."

Call me crazy, but the more the voice spoke, the more I felt that I've been here before. Wherever she was. "Are you God?" I questioned, almost positive that I was actually hearing the voice of the Most High Himself.

"No, I am not God, but I am connected to the source. I am only here to show you the light."

"So, you're an angel?"

"No. I am you. At your highest degree. I am your conscience in its purest form. I am your spirit, that fills the energy of your soul. I was sent here to show you the way. You were sent here to make a life-changing decision."

"Show me the way? Why now? Where have you been all this time? And where do you expect me to go after this?"

"I was with you all along. Your lust, false desires, greed, envy, hate, and misunderstanding distracted you away from the guidance of the straight path. I only expect you to save us from the blazing fires of hell."

"How am I supposed to do that? Why couldn't you save us? How do I even know if heaven or hell is real if this is happening? And if I'm dead, then why am I not in one of those places?"

"All the answers to your questions are already known within you. If you dig deep enough, you will find all that you seek. It is impossible for me to save us by myself. For without you, I am only a lost soul. Same as you without me. You are not ready for the afterlife at this moment. Your life purpose has yet to be fulfilled."

"You have a choice to make between being initiated into the light or continuing to wonder through the darkness. Either way, your destiny shall be fulfilled. Whether it be favored in the eyes of the Most High or satisfying to the savage demands of your demons. That will work callously at separating you from your highest potential."

What will I have to do?" I didn't know what would happen next. I had no idea where to go from here. I just knew that I didn't want to remain here. When I used to watch people die in the movies, it was always that one person advising them not to enter the light. Now here I was talking to a voice trying to convince me that he was a part of me on another level. He was telling me that this light would evolve me into a higher spiritual being. A person who is able to find the right answers, tools, and direction. It was kind of hard to believe, but then again, what did I have to lose?

My intuition was telling me that the voice was sincere, honest, and trustworthy. The silence of my ego allowed me to feel, hear and understand my intuition louder and more clearly than ever.

"Well!" The voice that was beginning to sound like my own voice more and more, spoke again. "You could enter the light and become one with yourself and together we can fulfill our mission statement. Or you could remain here as I said before, alone, so dark that you won't even be able to find yourself."

"Where can I find this light?"

"It's inside of you."

"I can't see it." I couldn't even see my body. It was like I had no toes, fingers, arms, legs, or a body to contain an inside. It felt like I was everywhere while being nowhere at all.

"Open your eyes," I told myself, sounding just like the voice that I'd been talking to all the while. "Brace yourself. The illumination from the light is bright. Once you enter it, you will be awarded or punished for all your deeds. You will have an understanding of all the things to which you were once ignorant. You will be enlightened and heightened to a spiritual conscience. To revert back from this state of wisdom is to enter the corrupted world of no return."

For the first time in my death, I felt a part of my body. My eyes struggled to open. Eventually, I was blessed with vision. Combining rays of light shined down on me. I wanted to use my arm to block the light. I couldn't. I even tried to close my eyes back. I was unable to do that as well. I was like a deer stuck, staring at headlights.

I swear I thought I was tripping. That couldn't have been farther from the truth. I have seen an angel-like version of myself. He was transparent but visible. He was bright. He was big and getting bigger the closer he came. His presence was unharmful, peaceful, but powerful. I became face-to-face with myself. A better me.

He, or I, reached down and touched the temples of my head. I had an envision of my entire past life, beginning from the moment the bullet approached my head. It slowed down right before coming into contact. The bullet reversed its direction and sped up on its way back into the gun. The police officers stood back, and Flex approached. Everything was now moving faster, going backwards like a movie in rewind.

At one point in time, I was surrounded by all the people I killed, harmed, hurt, or disrespected. I relived the moments I had money and power. Then just like that, I was broke again. Before I knew it, I was back incarcerated, multiple times. The next thing I knew, I was a child again. Quickly after, it seemed as if the doctors were shoving me back into my mother's womb.

Time and everything moved by. It came to a sudden halt. Now at normal speed, everything resumed its natural order. The baby version of myself forced his little self back into the world. The first voice I heard outside of my current one was the sound of the baby me crying. The next sound was a constant beep. Then another, and another. Beep! Beep! Beep!

Once again, I was able to feel my body. It felt as if I was uncontrollably falling into space. It was like a trance-like experience that was aroused strongly by pleasure and ecstasy. A warm shimmering sensation throughout my entire body. My ghost took its hands off my temple and crawled into my chest. Just like that, I felt alive again. It was like I was reborn. I realized that I was lying in a hospital bed. I sat upright, erecting the top half of my body.

"Oh, my goodness." I heard a woman's voice expressed in awe. "He's up!"

"Three days in a coma is amazing for his condition." I now heard the voice of a male. "I was sure he would be out longer than that. In fact, I wasn't quite sure if he would make it back."

I comprehended the words I heard but was still a bit confused. He spent three days in a coma. It only seemed like I was gone for a matter of minutes. Nowhere near close to a day, let alone, three. Regardless of how many days it took, I was back!

Chapter 8: Flex's New Ward Order
Scene: Jackson Ward

A few days ago, I was able to collect the items from the back of Q's car. I had been transported to a safe duck-off spot at the Carter Ward on the One Way. To say that I was disappointed was an understatement. Do you know how pissed I was to find only one brick and a half, a couple of pounds of weed and some guns? I guess I had given my late brother a little bit too much credit.

I personally witnessed the number of bricks that went through our operation. Shit, it was safe to say that I moved the majority of them. To only end up with one brick and a half was completely embarrassing. After all the business we conducted, I wanted to give him the benefit of the doubt and say that he sold the missing bricks. Then I'll have to wonder about the missing money. We had gotten to the point where 100,000 was a normal income on a biweekly basis. For real, that shit wasn't a problem to me. You know Ima make shit shake.

When Q had fallen back for them a few weeks, it kind of caused a drought. It wasn't really anyone else to score from. All the other main sources in the projects went through Q. The little bit of shit I had, ran out quickly. Due to the high rate of popular demand, the streets were dry. Now I was back in commission.

That's what landed me here, in the Money House. Present was Big Dee; he was the honcho for the Bottom Boys. Hawk, who ran the Top Notch Hustla's. He was valuable, but I don't really trust him. And y'all already know Reggie. I was going over my plan with them. One, I really knew they couldn't afford to refuse even if they wanted to. The streets were desperate. Niggas were trying to eat. I decided to try out my plan starting with a quarter-brick. I proposed to front three ounces a piece to them in exchange for an agreement for everyone to bring all money back to the table.

I knew that niggas had become accustomed to moving heavier shit. Three ounces seemed like a slap in the face. If niggas wanted to find their way back to the top, they would have to start back at the bottom. Flat footing every dime or selling nothing over an eight-ball at a time for a higher price. I wanted to see every dollar moving. I wanted to control the economy. Since I had the product, I made the rules. Besides, I wanted to see who was willing to prove themselves to me. Who was willing to go against the grain causing shit to hit the fan?

"So, you mean to tell me that you want niggas to go back to nickel and dimes and bring you all da money?" Hawk asked. "Do you know how hot it is in des streets?" "12 locking up any and everything that has anything to do with us."

"That's what y'all got Soulja fo' dick." I reminded Hawk. "Get dem lil' niggas to help ya'll push. Put pressure on dem pigs. Make dem bitches scared to come out dis bitch."

"How we gone go to war with 12 and get money?" Big Dee asked a good question.

"Distractions, shit. We can lead the battle to one part of da projects causing a smoke screen while getting da Carter Ward back jumping. We can set up a no trespassing zone fo' da police around da border of da Carter Ward.

"All I need is for y'all to stick it out and stand yo' ground. At least til I come up with da next move. I think I gotta a way that we can get in some of those greedy pigs' pockets. That way, we'll be able to do as we please. First, though, we have to let dem know that we ain't none to play with."

"I'm down for whatever," Reggie declared. "Especially when it comes to da hood. On some real shit though, I ain't even been able to function since a pussy took my nigga Q. It's been three days. A nigga ain't got back yet."

"I know brah. I feel you." I falsely agreed with Reggie. "We gone get da nigga responsible fo' dis shit. Everybody actin' like they don't know shit. It's only a matter of time before I start to take it out on anybody suspicious."

"What bout that black ass nigga?" Big Dee asked another good question. "Top Shotta."

"That's a good question brah." I fed Big Dee's wonderment. "I went through da South to check with him and see what he knew about Q's last moves. Da nigga was gone. No sign of him. Like he packed everything up and left. So, yeah, dude definitely suspect turned potential vic."

"I'ma kill that nigga if I find out he had something to do with that shit." Reggie was speaking through clenched teeth with his famous mug on his face.

"Da more I think about it; he is startin' to sound like da most logical person behind dis," I said as I really thought to myself. Why didn't I think of this at first? I could make that nigga take all the blame for my brother's murder. I ain't know that nigga from a can of paint. He was just a stray dog to me. Someone that my brother knew from his past and took in to hide him from his troubles. "Someone close, but not in da circle," I uttered.

"Exactly." Big Dee simply agreed.

"We need to find that nigga," Reggie said with his eyebrows curled up from expressing anger.

"That's a lock," I asserted.

"I knew I should have never fucked wit ya'll niggas," Hawk said falling way off topic.

"What?" I asked, really wanting to know the meaning behind his statement.

"I'm just saying," he just said. "I had my own thing going. Going good at that. Then it was like ya'll forced me or manipulated me into fuckin' with ya'll on some state property get down or lay down type shit."

"We ain't force you to do shit Hawk," I reminded him. "You had a choice." I'll admit, at one point in time we were aiming to kill Hawk. He even had Q shooting at his head. But Hawk was the type of person, if he wasn't with you, then he was a vicious threat.

"Shidd, I can't tell." He disagreed. "Y'all be tryin' to convince da whole hood to blackball me. If I hadn't agreed to link up, I'd probably be dead right now." He was most likely right.

Now you were probably seeing why I wasn't willing to trust him. He was like a two-headed snake. Indecisive and ready to switch sides at any given moment. "So, what's yo point Hawk?" I wanted to know. "You with us or naw?"

"I mean once again, it looks like I don't have a choice."

"Once again, you definitely have a choice. Ride or die."

"You know I'm riding fool."

I would have to keep a face in the back of my head around this fool. He showed all the signs of betrayal. Trust me, I know a snake when I see one. Don't trip though, the moment he found himself with a sweet tooth, I'll already have a cake baked for him.

Chapter 8: Q's Interrogation
Scene: The Hospital

The very next day after coming out of what the doctors called a coma, the Richmond Police Department's homicide detectives were by my bedside. Still to this day, handcuffs remained tight around my wrist. Leaving me chained to the bed. I appreciated the second chance at life that was given to me, but I knew that I would have to fight even harder for my freedom.

I was almost certain that these two detectives were not here to free me. One being Black and the other White, really made no difference. I wasn't new to the system. I already knew how the game went.

"Good morning Mr. Anderson." The Black detective spoke first. "Well, I'll understand if your morning wasn't as good as mine. I woke up to a beautiful wife. Made love to her followed by a nice hot shower. You smell like a piece of shit by the way. Soon after, I ate a nice size breakfast with a hot cup of coffee followed by a good morning cigarette. Yet, here you are, handcuffed to a bed with a bandage wrapped around your head. Smelling like you haven't taken a shower in weeks. Excuse me for being so rude. My name is Detective Graham."

I don't know what the fuck dude was talking about. I was having the best morning of my life. I woke up this morning with the sun shining in my face through the window. Taking in a breath of air through my lungs was a blessing all within itself. On top of all of that, I had this bad little nurse running in and out of the room catering to me. She fed me pain reliever pills, food, and the best part of all, ice-cold water. I was having a wonderful morning.

"Please Mr. Anderson," now the White detective was speaking his peace. "Excuse my partner. My name is Detective Brandon Black. You can just refer to me as Black if that makes you comfortable."

Hold up. First of all, I found it funny that the Black detective was named after a cracker, a brown cracker at that. Then there was a White detective standing here telling me to call him Black. This shit was really deeper than the surface.

Graham was a Black racist that hated his own race. Black was a White boy who probably tried to be Black all his life. He thought he was the cool one. Together, their ying-yang matched perfectly. A complete mixture of two confused intellectuals. I'm not sure how many years of practice these two held under their belts. But I had to give it to them. They had this good cop bad cop shit down pack so far. The only problem was that they had the wrong suspect this time. I don't know shit. I didn't do shit. And that's what I was sticking with.

"We were hoping that you would be willing to answer a few questions for us," Black admitted. "Depending on how honestly you answer the questions will determine how much you help both us and you out," I said nothing. They waited.

"Hello dick head," Graham teased, "What the fuck, are you deaf?" I exercised my right to remain silent. "This bastard must be fucking brain dead," Graham continued with his insults.

"Listen Mr. Anderson," Black took over again. "We under-stand if you're not in the mood to talk. However, it's looking like you are up against a heavy storm. We're not here to stir up water. At least try to bring some type of calmness to your world."

I wasn't trying to hear that shit. I was calm. I ain't gone lie though, this fucking Graham cracker was starting to piss me off a little. Even discrimination from my own race couldn't break me. I was from the trenches. I see that shit every day where I'm from. I will not fold.

I definitely had my mind made up about holding my water. With that, I needed a constructive plan. I had no idea where to start. I had no support. No lawyer, money, or contacts. The few people that I thought may help me out, I had no way of reaching out to them. The guys and I were changing phone numbers so frequently that it was hard to remember just one.

Things were so fucked up right now that I wasn't even sure if anybody knew I was alive.

"You know what Mr. Anderson?" Graham asked me. "You are a disgrace to your race." "Look who's talking?" I asked myself. I found it funny how he said, 'your race' and not ours.

"You are fucking worthless. Your life isn't even worth a rusty penny. I wish your stupid ass would have died days ago. I waited wasted days for you to come through only to drag your ass up here for nothing. With the time and charges you're facing, you are going to wish that you took this chance to snitch like your other nigger friends. Come on Black, let's leave this piece of shit to rot."

Did that nigga just call me a nigger? His ass was four tonnes blacker than me. Looked like somebody deep-fried his ass and left him there. He was hot too. If he were White, his face would be plush red. But since he's not, I think he turned purple. I wanted to call his ass a cracker. I think he would have taken that as a compliment.

"Before we go Mr. Anderson, I want to leave you, my card. If you at any moment have a change of heart or something comes to mind, anything, please give me a call. I'll leave the card here on the desk," Black implied. That was not the type of contact I needed. They were gone.

As soon as I thought I would be able to return to my peace of mind, I found out that I was wrong. Detective Graham walked back into the room alone. I couldn't predict what he wanted. I tried to pay him no mind as if he weren't even there. He made that impossible by walking up to me and squeezing the handcuffs on my wrist as tight as my bone would allow.

I ain't gone lie, that shit was hurting to the point that I couldn't take it anymore. With my free hand, I gripped the wrist of the detective and tried to pull his hand off my wrist. That probably was a bad decision. He used his two-hand advantage to wrap the other one around my throat. The pressure he applied was working quickly to cut off the circulation to my windpipe. I gasped for air, released his wrist, and took a swing towards his face as best I could. It landed, but barely. It only pissed him off more.

"Listen here you little piece of shit," Detective Graham scolded. Now with both of his hands wrapped aggressively tight around my neck, "If I wanted to, I could kill you myself. I can't count on both our hands combined how many times I've gotten away with murder. I suggest you get with the fucking program."Of course, I didn't reply. I couldn't. Instead, I stared into his eyes without a blink. I feared that I was on the verge of experiencing my second death this week.

Chapter 9: Flex's Next Move
Scene: Jackson Ward

Business was once again booming in the Metropolitan. Well, at least around Jackson Ward, it was. I ain't have enough shit to flood the whole city yet. That was a problem. I was already having small anxiety attacks. This pressure was heavier than I thought. On top of that, I have the tendency to snap out when shit doesn't go the way I expect. I had to make sure that didn't happen.

We sat four deep in a car parked on First Street in Jackson Ward. Wolf operated the steering wheel sitting in the driver's seat. He was the best driver of all of us present. The little flunky started off as a car thief. In the back seat were Lil' Mark and Blu. Just in case y'all forgot, Lil' Mark was like my right hand. Blu was a member of the Top Notch Hustla's with Hawk.

Word on the streets was that it was a nigger deeper in the northern part of the city pushing quite heavily for times like these. He had a shop set up in the Highland Park section of the North. I thought paying him a surprised visit would do justice to my own selfish needs. One way or another, this whole city would be mine.

Scene 2: Highland Park

We pulled up on Meadow Bridge around Highland Park. The sun was getting out of our way at the perfect time, ducking below the horizon, darkening the sky.

"What's da plan Flex?" Blu asked me.

"Stick to da script," I replied making sure I had a bullet waiting in the chamber of my Glock .40. "Wolf, hold da car down. Keep it running. We poppin' in and out." "Lil Mark!" I called out now peeking through the rear-view mirror.

"Yoo.." was his response.

"Spare nothing."

"Got you fool."

I hopped out of the car and crept to the back of an alley. Lil' Mark and Blu followed. Gun in hand, I stepped to the back door of the targeted house. Approaching the unguarded door, I wasted no time trying to twist the knob. With one powerful kick, I knocked that bitch off the hinges. The door swung open allowing us access to the kitchen. It was the perfect spot.

A couple of niggas were caught by surprise but still made an attempt to grab guns and rush. Bow! Bow! I popped the first nigga that ran up. Dropping him to the floor. Two more niggas followed in his footsteps carrying pistols. The guns were no match for the AR-15 that Lil' Mark shot from his hand. The bullets entered both of their bodies. Rattling them like a baby toy.

We bulged into the kitchen. "Lil' Mark, watch da back door. Blu, make sure niggas don't come in dis kitchen." I removed the bag from over my shoulder and started filling that bitch up with every valuable item in sight. On the table sat drugs, guns, and money. I wanted them all. I searched through the cabinets, drawers and even the refrigerator hoping to run into more products.

I was beginning to regret only bringing one bag. This bitch was damn near full already. As I was stuffing the final items into the bag, a gang of niggas were pulling up to the back door. Lil' Mark did his part at keeping them at a distance. But them niggas were deep like roaches. I upped the Glock, discharging the gun on my way out the door. Fuck that. I was not getting trapped in this trap house. I had to make it out.

The rivals were put on the defense quickly. Not knowing how to handle the pressure, they started to scatter like the very roaches they imitated. "Let's go! Let's go!" I yelled out to Lil' Mark and Blu who were chasing down the opps by sending bullets flying behind them.

We packed the car and before the doors were fully closed, Wolf was smashing the gas. Straggling shooters spilled from side houses and alleys spitting shots at our speeding car. Lil' Mark and Blu took joy in returning fire by halfway hanging out of the back windows. Wolf did his job and got us out of there safely.

Chapter 10: Keyshia's Suspicion
Scene: Workplace

Something just wasn't right. This wasn't normal. I could feel it. You know the feeling of death? I'm pretty sure you do. We all have experienced it at least once in our life in some type of way. Other times I've lost a person close to me, it always felt like that person had taken a piece of me with them. For some strange reason, it didn't feel like that with Q. It felt like he was still fully connected to me like he was still here.

You're probably thinking a bitch crazy right? But you see it. You were right there on the murder scene with me. Unless you know something that I don't. We both witnessed Q's lifeless body balled up in the streets. Ok, let me clear up my reason for suspicion. I know I'm not fucking crazy. First of all, Q had just dropped off a quarter of a million dollars right before he exited out my back door. I said that to say that I was trying to get my ex future husband burned days ago. The money was far from the problem. The problem was finding the body to bury. To my understanding, no one had reached out in an attempt to identify the body. The only family that Q had was his brother, daughters, and me. The hospitals claimed that they did not have anybody by the name of DeQuan Anderson. I'm not sure why, but I even checked in with all of the surrounding jails. None of them held Q there. Now, do you see why this shit was so suspicious?

Deep down inside of me, I prayed that my eyes really did tell me a lie. I hoped that Q somehow had another chance at life like those gangsters in the movies or urban novels. I know that shit was far-fetched though. If I hadn't lost my mind by now, I surely was on my way. One thing I knew for sure was that this was not a movie. And it damn sure wasn't a book. If it were, the Author would probably make me some spoiled rich hustler's wife. Or a whore being pimped by a millionaire. Not on this planet. Definitely not Keyshia Johnson.

"Um, excuse me Miss Johnson. I appreciate the gesture, I really do, but umm." When I snapped out of my daydream like a trance, I remembered that I had a handful of wrinkled old man's balls in my hands.

"Oh my God. I'm so sorry, I…"

"No, it's ok. I can tell that you've been kind of out of it these past few days. Just clean me up so I can get ready for my nap." That was my patient. I was a CAN nurse, so cleaning old men's balls was nothing new. I was just glad that the old man didn't get the wrong impression. One thing that he was right about, was that I was in no type of working condition. I had to get to the bottom of my suspicion. It was like Q had just upped and disappeared. Like a ghost.

Chapter 11: Q's Quagmire
Scene: The Hospital

Lord, please help me through this situation. I know it seems like I was just in your presence not too long ago but… "I'll fucking kill you. You Black bastard. You stupid son of a bitch." As if choking me half to death wasn't enough, this police ass nigga even interrupted my silent prayer.

I started to relax some and just allowed the universe to take its course. If snitching was my purpose for a second chance at life, then you could send me back to the darkness. Soon, I felt like that's exactly where I was headed back to. The feeling was all too familiar. "That's right you little bitch, go to sleep," Detective Graham insisted.

Knock, knock, knock. Someone was at the door of the hospital room. That gave me hope to fight for a few more seconds.

Whoever it was wasted no time entering the room. "Excuse me." I was happy to hear a woman's voice. "Is everything ok in here?" I knew it was my nurse.

Detective Graham quickly unleashed his bear claws from around my neck. I was finally able to replenish my lungs with the proper portion of air needed. "Yes, umm… Nurse Porter. Everything is fine. Mr. Anderson and I were just having a… discussion. Right, Mr. Anderson?" I wasn't about to agree with that fuck boy even if he was telling the truth. "Ok, Mr. Anderson. I guess we can pick up this conversation when we meet again." For the second time, Detective Graham was gone. Before he could fully step past the door seal, I was already praying that he wouldn't make a third entrance.

It seemed like demons were attacking me from every corner of my life. I don't know if I was being repaid for the sins of my evils or if the devil himself had a bounty out on my head. Whichever one it was, I felt overpowered. Like there was absolutely nowhere for me to hide.

"Are you ok?" Nurse Porter asked me coming closer to my bedside. I said nothing while using my free hand to rub the throat area of my neck. "Your eyes are bloodshot red," she informed me of what I couldn't see but could feel.

The pretty, short, caramel skin tone nurse placed her soft hand on mine. "Move your hand! Let me see your neck!" she demanded nicely. All the while removing my hand herself. The touch of her hand put me in a calm submissive type of ease. The care she provided always seemed to wash away all of my troubles. "What did he do to you?" she asked, only seeming half shocked. "Your throat is terribly bruised." She leaned in closer to examine my neck and eyes.

To think, a minute ago, my mind was focused on life or death. Now my focus was on these two titties that dangled in my face through her pretty pink and purple butterfly nurse uniform top. I used my imagination to try to think of what they would look like uncovered. Judging off that conversation I had with myself during my moment of death, I would have thought that my lustful desires would have died. I now knew that I was mistaken. My flesh was still weak. My nose was aroused by her scent. The hairs on my skin stood up from the touch of her hands. My ears were even turned on from the vibrations of her voice. My eyes undressed her while my mind fucked her.

Leave it to my dick head to reveal all my thirsty emotions. Through the hospital gown and sheets, I had become erect. I was so caught up in my own fantasy, that I almost didn't notice the Pitbull standing up. That was until Nurse Porter accidentally brushed up against him with her elbow. She looked down in the direction of my tool and was slightly startled. She stood up but stayed. I stared into her dark-hazed eyes. If it was possible, I kind of felt embarrassed and prideful at the same time.

"Mr. Anderson," Nurse Porter said but no words followed after. Then, as if it just hit her, she looked down to the bottom of her pretty shirt. It was wet. I mean soaking wet. "Oh my God!" she said but remained calm. I think the 'oh my God' was more for me than her. "You are fucking bleeding nonstop," she now noticed my wrist but didn't touch it. "What did that ass hole do to you?" Right now, I was undefeated when it came to not answering questions. Seems like the more I didn't answer, the more that came.

"Excuse me for one minute Mr. Anderson. You are going to need stitches. I'm going to get a doctor." I thought the saying was 'snitches get stitches.' My whole world was upside down.

Chapter 12:   Flex Brings it Home
Scene: The Money House

"Ayee, no bullshit. I ain't had rec like that in a minute. We need to do that shit again." I was sitting at the table with Wolf, Lil' Mark and Blu. I was happy as a bitch for real. I mean, of course, I had that 300,000 that I got from Q, but that was between you and me. I expected it to stay that way.

Anyway, them folks across the bridge in Highland Park were actually playing with a little something. I snatched up a little over 65,000 in cash value. A few guns that I would put in the streets for throw-away murder weapons. I found one pound of weed. I'm assuming that was the personal sack for their trap. I went to bust that shit down and sell it too. The only problem was that we rolled a blunt of that shit up to discover the gas. I need to find out where they copped that shit from. My most prized possession was the three-and-a-half bricks I snatched up. We caught them bitches at a good time too. They were just about to hit the lab and start the process.

This lick gave me a big boost. A little room to breathe and time to scheme further. Until then, I was prepared to move these bricks to the kitchen which was actually another apartment in the Carter Ward. That's where all the cooking went down. It was time to eat and turn the hood up again. I was anxious to see the piles of money flowing in. Ima show you niggas how to ball out. By the time I'm finished, they will call me the Big Meech of Richmond. Free him by the way.

Self Made Tay

Chapter 13: Q's Departure
Scene: Hospital

In less than half an hour, the doctor had me stitched up. The metal from the handcuffs had cut into the skin around my wrist. It was really worse than I thought. Then again, what could be worse than my situation? Don't bother to answer. If it's worse than this shit, I'd rather refuse to hear about it.

This was the first time all day that I was finally able to get the room to myself. Usually, I would prefer to be alone. However, sitting in silence allowed time for my thoughts to haunt me. As much as I tried not to think about it, a major part of me felt like I needed to know. Out of all people, why him? Why Flex? My own and only blood brother. Did I not do all that I could for that nigga? Did I not give him all that he wanted and more? Did that fool not know that I loved him unconditionally?

From the thought of the love I had for Flex a lone, tear sneaked from my eye. The pain hurt worse than the bullet that plugged my head. I kind of felt this shit coming. My biggest mistake was expecting it from my enemies. I will never forget the look on that nigga's face. I could relate to how Eve felt when the serpent slid up on her in the Garden of Eden. That nigga popped me like I was the opps. Dropping me like a dog with rabbis in the streets.

I didn't want to think about that shit right now. Let alone dwell on it. I pushed the power button on the remote control to turn the TV on. The channel was already stationed on Channel 8 news. The deaths of Tall and Short were still the top topic. As if I never existed, there was no mention of me. No hints of my whereabouts. Not even any suspicion of my involvement. Nothing. Like I was never here. Like I was the ghost that I always claimed to be.

I was just about to change the channel before I noticed the news reporter was changing the topic. I saw a very familiar house on the TV. It was on Meadow Bridge Road in Highland Park. I knew that house because it belonged to Low and his crew. It was their main and biggest trap house in that part of the city. For some reason, a massive shootout erupted surrounding the house leaving five dead and three injured. Low was one of my latest customers. Through him, I had planned to monopolize Highland Park. It struck an interest in me to figure out the motive behind the massacre.

That's when it hit me. Regardless of your condition, life goes on. I could no longer sit here searching for pity. Acting dead while having the opportunity to live.

With the handcuffs switched to my other hand, I used my injured hand to rub the inch-long hairs on my chin. Something was telling me something. I just couldn't figure out what.

"Mr. Anderson," Nurse Porter came through the door saving me from going crazy due to isolation. "Are you feeling better?"

"A lil bit. Thanks to you," I replied dryly.

"You don't sound happy at all. What's wrong?" Nurse Porter was pretty and smart too. Still, I wondered how many college courses she had to go through to figure that out.

"Naw, I'm blessed. I guess."

"You guess?" she asked me playfully. "I personally think that you have more than enough to be thankful and happy about Mr. Anderson."

"Could you please not call me Mr. Anderson anymore?" I politely asked the nurse. "You can call me DeQuan."

"Well excuse me DeQuan." She smiled and giggled a little. "And since I can't call you Mr. Anderson, you can't call me nurse, Ms. Nurse, or Nurse Porter anymore."

"I don't know yo name though."

"My name is Sha'Mayne."

"Ok, Ms. Sha'Mayne."

"No," she stopped me. "Just Sha 'Mayne." Nurse Porter was taking steps closer to my bedside. Closing the little space that was left between us. Surprisingly, she placed her soft hand on my rough, ashy, and wounded one.

"DeQuan," she spoke my name with a soft, seductive, yet saddened tone. "I know that you are going through so much right now and I hate to be the bearer of bad news. However, I wanted to be the one to tell you first. Sort of give you a head start. I'm pretty sure that you were expecting this outcome anyway, but sometime today, they will be transporting you out of the hospital and down to the city jail." Verbally, I said nothing but I'm pretty sure that my facial expression spoke volumes. Of course, I knew I was going to jail. I'd been on the run for over a month now. The expression on my face wasn't due to the obviously stated news, but for her motive of feeling the need to tell me in advance.

"Earlier, I overheard those two detectives plotting to charge you with false and trumped-up charges." That was already expected as well, I thought to myself. "I heard them saying all these horrible things about you that I just couldn't imagine. They even called you a cop killer, mass murderer, and kingpin." Well, at least one of those titles was true.

"Anything you want to know about me, you can ask me. If I feel comfortable enough, I may answer. But never believe what you hear about me." I made myself clear.

"I don't believe anything that the police say period. And I definitely can't see the things they said about you being true. You are a beautiful person. You have a beautiful body, a beautiful soul, and a heart so powerful that I can see it beating through your chest." She placed her free hand on my chest over my heart. The beat from my heart intensified. I also had a tensed awakening growing in my manhood.

"DeQuan, I don't know the things that you've been through, and it seems as if you have even more problems to deal with ahead of you. Something inside of my head is screaming to help you. I don't know what I can do, except this." The nurse hurriedly went into her breast and pulled out a sandwich bag full of the same pain pills that she had been feeding me during my stay here. "You cannot get caught with these," she reached over my body and placed the pills under the small of my back. "If you do, that's my ass."

"When you get to the jail, they are going to downgrade your prescription to Tylenol. This should hold you over for a nice time.

Please don't abuse them." As she was coming back up into her stance, it happened again. Only this time, it was her open palm that got a swipe at my shaft. If I was dumb, I would have thought that it was a mistake. Being that I was smarter than that, I knew that she knew exactly what she was doing.

"Oops, I'm sorry!" She apologized. "Why does that keep happening?" I thought she asked me, but she was staring down at my dick, through the sheets, as if she had x-ray vision. Talking to my little man.

"I think it's swollen," I joked seriously.

"I think you're right. I also think that you have a secret thing for me." I don't think that my thing was a secret anymore. "Let me help you with that." Nurse Porter pulled the sheets over to uncover my body. She dug underneath my hospital gown and straddled my balls with her soft moisturized hands. I could have busted a nut just from her messaging my sack. That didn't last long.

I knew I wasn't sleeping. This was far from a dream. The nurse leaned over the bed and slowly filled her mouth with my manhood. The combination of her soft tongue and wet lips caused me to moan in pleasure. Before I knew it, Shawty was getting wicked in a heavenly way. She twisted and turned my dick, all head motion. She sucked and slobbed like she was trying to prevent any evidence from staining the sheets.

At the beginning, I was watching as my dick entered in and out of her face. Soon though, I had to lay back and close my eyes. My toes curled as I felt my dick head being crowded with built-up sperm. It wasn't long before they were busting out. I never saw them. I found out the nurse had a side profession. She sucked on my dick head until she emptied it out. Swallowing every drop of sperm down her throat. Felt like I had died and gone to heaven. No bullshit.

Chapter 14: Flex the Outlaw
Scene: Lil Shawty's Crib

Shawty had me gone for real. I won't let her know that though. I know for a fact that I had her gone though. Say she never had a nigga like me. She had the best head I've ever had in my life. No bullshit. Shawty had me suckatized with the head. Plus, the fact that the bitch was a 12 made it even sweeter. Talking about being above the law, I was standing over this bitch right now. Cramming my dick down her throat, holding her ponytail. Shawty so wide she be letting me smack her ass in the face and all that while she sucked the dick. Straight freak. Bad too.

She had a brown sugar complexion. Hair dropped down to her shoulders. She had these crazy-ass olive-green eyes. Soft ass gummy worm lips. All natural. So, washer body, bouncing boobs, awesome ass. This bitch even had a four-pack in her stomach.

Right now, I had this bitch on her knees stroking her face. I was looking for another reason to smack her ass. So, I wiggled my shaft around in her mouth looking for a tooth to scrape on. Not once did she allow that to happen. Finding ways to adjust her mouth to avoid contact. I grabbed her by the back of the neck and forced her to deep-throat this dick. She took it like a champ. "Ugghh.." Without warning, I sent slime sliding down her throat. This shit felt so good. I almost collapsed on the bitch. She gagged a bit which was rare. I pulled my dick out of her mouth and tumbled down on the couch.

It looked like she was trying to catch her breath. I hoped she did. Can't let that head go to waste. Once she did, she climbed up on the couch and lay underneath me. She grabbed my dick, which was twice the size of her hand, and squeezed it tight as she wanted to. "What, you tryna' to kill me nigga?"

"Aaahh..!! Bitch! Wat da fuck you doing?"

"Shut up nigga for I pull dis shit out da socket. Why da fuck you ain't tell me you were cumin?"

"I tried to hold it in." I played dumb.

"Stupid. I'm not talking bout dat. I know da face you make when you are about to cum. I'm talkin' bout why you ain't tell me you were about to cum ova here? I told you bout poppin' up." Lil Shawty was strict with her rules. Real discreet. She would hate for her parents to find out that their twenty-something-year-old baby girl was fucking with a gangster. On top of that, her job. Imagine if they found out that their trusted officer was fucking with a real street nigga?

I met Shawty at a party near the campus of VCU College. I was on her ass as soon as I saw her. Shit, every nigga in that bitch. But I was the one and only me, she chose, and I did what I do. Come to find out this bitch was the police. As soon as I figured it out, I put it to use. That's how I got that video on Tim telling ass a while back. That was something small. Just a test. Now that I knew she was down, I was ready to turn her up.

She never had a street nigga before. I had to recalibrate her way of thinking. Somebody told her that all street niggas were the bad guys. Who the fuck said some dumb ass shit like that? That's like saying all police are good. Anyway, now that she understood the way we think and lived, I had her eating out the palms of my hands. "I need you to get yo people in check. Put dem pigs in some type of order. Fo' I send dey ass to da slaughterhouse." I was already beginning the process of rolling a blunt.

"How da fuck am I posed to do that?" She was facing me fixing her ponytail, uniform on and all the accessories.

"You better figure it out."

"Boy, yo ass is crazy. Yo ass gone get me killed."

"What, you wouldn't die for me?" She stared at me trying to figure out if I was serious or not. I smirked.

Chapter 15: Q's Care
Scene: Richmond City Jail

After being dropped off at the jail, I was searched and processed and searched again. I ended up in the medical section. All alone once again. I was good though. I think I wanted to be alone. Or maybe I was just getting used to it. I kind of wanted to go to the population. See who I would run into. Get some food and proper hygiene. Reach out to the streets. I know I had taken a bullet to the head, but I questioned the decision to be placed on the medical tier. You know I've been here before. Do you know how many times inmates were thrown into the population with fresh war wounds? Me neither. Too many. Like I said though, I was good.

Nurse Porter was right. The nurses in the jail tried to overdose me with Tylenol. I was happy as a bitch that I was able to get the pills through processing. Don't ask me how. Just know that the chances were slim to none. One of them with a couple of Tylenols set me straight. I was literally numb to pain.

I had the TV to myself. The showers, toilets, and sinks. The tables and too many bunks for one person to sleep on. I was laid back on three stacked jail mats, a self-made pillow, and a level for my feet. The food was trash. But I was so high that I ain't give a fuck. Plus, it was only me. I was a lock for a double portion. No matter my misfortunes, my mind was still set on king mode.

It's been over a week now. I guess. I really wasn't counting. My days turned into nights. My nights were spent reiterating my resurrection, relaxing, and reading. Ironically, I had run through a couple of books by Sistah Soulja titled A Moment of Silence and Life After Death. Only God could explain to you how much I needed those reads at a time such as this. A few other urban novel authors kept me entertained for a few days like Nikki Turner, Kwan, Ca$h, and some new dude by the name of Romell Tokes. The readings were good, but only reminded me of the life that I was missing. The life that landed me here in the first place. The life I now desired to change.

I picked up a small one with the cover ripped off. I opened the book and read The Secret by Rhonda Byre. It was a short read, but powerful. The words tapped into a nerve of mine that made me want to change my life right at the moment. From there, I had an unquenched thirst to acquire knowledge of the mind. The power of your intentions, your words, and your actions. My next read was by Michael Eric Dyson. Immediately, he became one of my favorites.

Even now, I was struggling to stay awake, trying to read. As my energy went down, the sun was coming up. I closed the book and let my mind wander until I drifted off into a dream.

Chapter 16: Dawn's Mornings
Scene: Her Workplace

"Ugghh…" I hated the taste of vomit in my mouth. Seeing the contents of my stomach gushing into the commode, made me sicker, and the smell, ugh. I flushed the toilet and pathetically limped over to the sink. When I made it to the mirror, I looked into it. I looked terrible. Don't get it twisted. I was a bad bitch, or beautiful. Triple B, whichever one you feel like calling me. I was able to see beyond my eyes. My soul was aching. My body hurting from long nights of working the graveyard shift. Energy drained from sleepless days. I hated this job.

I wasn't sure how long I would be able to work here. My body was getting heavier to carry. I had gained at least 15 pounds by now. The few that noticed my weight change, loved it. Said it looked good on me. I agreed. My concern was how fast it was happening and how far it would go.

I was already two months. And already, I experienced so much pain, that I dreaded the seven long months to come. I swear, if Q weren't dead, I'd probably kill him myself. At times, this pain was to die for.

It was mainly the sickness. Almost every morning around this time, I would catch a stomach ache, become faint and regurgitate. This baby was putting me through hell already. With all the things going on with my body, it made it hard for me to shake my ass all night. Popping pussy was my provider. Knowing that I had a child on the way made me want to hustle harder. Every day, that ambition became harder to strive off. I know Q left me with a little cash, but we are talking about taking care of a human being for a lifetime. I'd be damned if I let my child experience my same struggles. Have to choose my choices and relive my realities.

I had a little under thirty minutes left to work around with this thong up my ass. Lately, I would be creeping up out of here before dawn. I hated sitting in this locker room at the end of my shift. Listening to bitches throw shade at each other, sharing secondhand smoke. Most of these hoes were intoxicated and ingenious which lead to a fucked-up combination of infringement. I basically bonded my business when it came to these bitches. These bugs knew not to come for the boss.

I've been stripping, dancing, entertaining, or whatever you want to call it for over a year now. It started as a means to pay my tuition for college. Somehow, I drifted into a delusional dream that I could do this shit forever. I understand the pain of Diamond from Players Club. That was one of my favorite movies by the way. I kind of envied Diamond in my unbalanced mind. At least she got to dance around a bunch of players. While I was the main attraction of a broke nigga ball.

In college, I was studying to become a defense attorney. It was hard and expensive, but my passion for the career drove me to conquer my doubts. It all started with my father. He always pushed me to be whatever I wanted to be. Well, after he was convicted to a life sentence on drug charges that he honorably took for a lifetime friend. My passions were doubled.

Paying for a lawyer, commissary and court fees forced me to put my tuition on the back burner. At first, I planned for it to only be temporary. That temporary turned into a whole year. And now, here I am. Got me and my unborn baby shaking ass on a stage, naked.

It was impossible to think about the baby without thinking of Q. He reminded me of my father so much. My father was a hood nigga, but I wasn't from the hood at all. By the time I was born, my father was straight, legit, and out of the game. Again, don't get the shit twisted, the hood was running all through my veins. All my life, I tried to avoid and deny it. Then I looked up one day and found myself in a homeless shelter for a couple of months. That's how I ended up in Jackson Ward. After experiencing being homeless on the street and then in a shelter, I said fuck school. Making getting money my first priority. My pockets were alright, but I know for a fact that I was born to be rich. These dollars were pennies to me. But still, though, pennies added up too.

I had to get myself out of this situation. Get back to my mission of freeing my father and preparing for my child to enter this world. I wish all that could be done just as easily as I just said it. In reality, my feet were killing me, this smoke was giving me a headache, and my heart was empty. I had the slightest clue as to where I could find the strength to control my willpower. All I knew is that I needed that energy badly and fast. Lord, please send me an angel. I just wanted to wake up in the morning on cloud nine as if I was in Heaven.

Self Made Tay

Chapter 17: Flex's Fuel
Scene: Jackson Ward

"Main, ya'll niggas out here bullshittin.' In da way ass niggas." I was pissed the fuck off.

"How we bullshittin'?" Red channeled in. "Dat Maine was lockin' and 12 ran down. It wasn't our fault."

"It is ya'll fault because if ya'll niggas listen to wat da fuck I tell you, den sit could go smooth." The police had just locked Hawk up not too long ago. The last thing I needed was to start the season of fall off with fallen-off troops. "Wat dey locked him up fo'?"

"Say he had warrants." Red was another member of TNH. Blu's right-hand man. "He ain't got none on him though. He was clean."

Before this, shit was actually going well this week. The money was picking up and it seemed like the police were starting to fall back. We had rolled up on a couple more licks over on the west end of the city. Them niggas were acting like they weren't a part of the city. I wanted to make sure they felt this drought like every other hood.

Skirttt... Cars' tires piled on the corner of St. John Street heading in our direction. Police cars ambushed us from both ends of the block. I had a pocket full of rocks and my Glock on me. I'd rather go to hell with my pops and brother before I got locked back in a cage. Forever, I will remain untainted.

Bow!! Bow!! Bow!! Bow!! I don't know what the rest of these niggas were waiting for. I ain't care to ask either. I squeezed the trigger of my gun releasing ether. Projectiles exploded escaping the chamber, exiting through the muzzle. They entered the windshield of the leading car shattering the glass. You would have thought with all that going on, they would at least pull up in bulletproof. How disrespectful?

I was a little way away from the one way where we had set up the no trespassing zone. I had a better chance of making it to a cul-de-sac at the end of St. John Street. We had code-named it 'O-

Block.' Its original nickname was the chilly willy hole. It sat at the bottom of a short steep hill and formed a circle of project buildings, back allies, and woods leading to a train track. I got the code name from the Chicago rappers representing Chi-Raq. In my mind, the O stood for omnipotent. That's what I was, omnipotent. The O-block was my oubliette. My intents were to outdraw the attention from the One-Way, to cause an obstruction on O-block. The location was the perfect setting for the objection. The chilly willy hole basically had no outlets. This allowed us to outfox the law or simply push them back up the hill if they attempted to intrude.

Oh shit! A bullet had flown past my head causing the vibrations of speeding wind to creep into my ear. Trying to kick it with y'all right now had my focus all the way thrown off. Good thing, my dog Lil' Mark was on point with his index finger. He was throwing shots like this shit was a bar fight. Never dropping the lifted pistol, I focused my aim on a cop that was taking shots at his opp. Bow!! One to the head dropped him like the casket he would soon be burned in.

The blood of the police officer escaped through the hole in his head, causing a leakage to spill out into the streets. His gang of police partners seemed shocked. I don't know what the fuck they thought. Those days of them spinning the block and niggas acting defenseless were over. Enslavement was abolished due to the emancipation proclamation. There was no more need for slave patrol best known as police. From this point on, at least in this city, we would govern ourselves. I don't give a fuck about what a news reporter told you. This collection of poverty and oppression was systematic. You niggas probably walking around sleeping. But I know for a fact that these days and times were only another form of the same shit that our ancestors went through instead of forcing us the way they did our forefathers. They misled us with tricks, trials, brainwashing, and domesticating.

Maine fuck! I swung my pistol left, squeezed twice, and dropped one. Swung back right and let off three more, dropping two. In my mind, I was cursing Red bitch ass out for running off leaving us with one less soldier to fight this battle. I'll have to deal with that nigga later. Right now, I was running over to a lying Lil' Mark who was stretched out on the ground behind a car. He was just standing behind the car only seconds ago.

I saw the whole thing like a slow-motion replay. Lil' Mark never had a chance to see it coming. The pig took aim and released the bullet from its shell. There was nothing I could do from there to stop it. The shit happened so fast that time wasn't a factor.

I crowded the remaining distance towards Lil' Mark and rested my back against the car. His eyes were still wide open and turning bloodshot red. He tried to reach for my shirt but was too weak to get a grip on it. I think he was trying to say something but the only sound that escaped his mouth was a gasp for air. Seconds later, I realized that he had just taken his last breath. He was no longer with us. Rest in Peace.

These mother fuckers just pulled the last straw out of my hand. Lil' Mark was my dog. I ain't talking about a fucking pet. He was my companion, my friend. If I had a heart, this moment would have taken a piece of it out. I felt worse for the loss of Lil' Mark than I did for my own brother. Aside from the fact that I was the one that took him out. Because if it were any other nigga that did, I would have kidnapped and tortured them. But Lil' Mark was a hundred percent for the hood. He was down for the cause, and obviously willing to die for this shit. For that, I respected him to the fullest. From the streets to the grave.

I removed the pistol from the hand of Lil' Mark and popped up like that joker in Jack in the box. I took aim with my left hand and used my peripheral to point right. None of this was thought out. Just pure killer instinct. At this point, I didn't care if I made it out of this jam. The way I see it, I was destined to fall at the same fate as my peers and the ones that came before me. Before that happens, I would make sure they will forever remember Flex. Shots back-to-back, flying out of two different guns at the same time from one person. My shots were so consistent that them bitches were scared to return fire. Instead, they took cover as

I swung the tools like a hammer trying to put the nails in the coffin.

I looked so small but felt bigger than I really was. As a matter of fact, everything looked small. It was like I was hovering above all the chaos that was taking place at this very moment. That experience didn't last long as I slowly returned to my body. That's when it hit me. I was still squeezing the triggers of the pistols while both of them gave off clicking sounds. Two extended thirty-shot clips are empty.

The same police that I tried to make victims out of, weren't scared anymore. Them fuckers were trying to toss me in a pan and fry me. I needed a way out but found myself stuck behind the same car that Lil' Mark laid behind. I looked Lil' Mark in his eyes which were still wide open. Before using my palm to close his eyelids. I made one last request. "Send me some help fool. Angels, demons. I don't give a fuck. Jus' help me make it out."

Seemed like help would never reach me. In this time of desperation, seconds felt like hours. I was stuck between a car and a corpse. All I heard was popping guns and bullets smacking the metal and glass of the car I was stuck behind. Suddenly, my call was answered. Leading the pack was Red followed by Blu, Wolf, Reggie, and a few other lifesaving demons. They all carried Draco's wasting no time, dumbing them like trash cans. As if that wasn't enough, Boss Baby, Big Baby, Burga, Big Dee, and a gang of others were spilling out of other cuts busting all types of guns.

I guess now all police had the same idea as me. The ones that weren't dead or brutally injured were trying their best to get the fuck out of here. Seeing them pack their cars and swerving away in an attempt to escape, filled my body with pride. You should have seen the shit. My niggas were chasing cars down the street actually running 12 out of the hood. This was the first rotation of turning tables.

I was on my way to O-block before the police could even make it off the street. I stumbled through the back door of an apartment and quickly tried to close it. Someone had intervened with that process by using their foot as a door stopper.

"Let us in bitch!" It was Blu and Reggie. I eased up on the door and allowed them to fall through.

"Lil' Mark," I said. They said nothing. Reggie closed and locked the door. He sat his back to the door and slid down to the floor. "How all of a sudden, dey snatch Hawk and then swarm da block da way dey did?" I asked snapping at no one in particular. "It doesn't take a rocket scientist to figure out wat jus' happened. As soon as I see dat bitch, Ima kill him."

Self Made Tay

Chapter 18: Let Hawk Tell It
Scene: The 4th Precinct

"You're a piece of shit. You know that right?" I hated this Uncle Tom oreo cookie-ass nigga Graham. He was always talking shit. I wanted to ask him if he knew that his breath smelled like shit. I'm talking about a whole bunch of shake that ass. "You really want me to believe that's all you know?"

"I told you Q ain't have beef wit nobody out here besides ya'll nigga happy nigga killin' ma' fucka's." Swop!! Graham smacked the shit out of me. I bet his bitch ass won't do that shit with these cuffs off. I'll ball his ass up. I know his crooked ass was up to something when he threw the cuffs on me without a real reason.

"What about you Hawkins?" Graham's partner Black asked.

"Wat bout me?"

I remember you and DeQuan having a problematic matter not too long ago. How did that turn out?"

"I ain't never had no problem wit dat man, especially nothin' worth killing him over." Graham and Black looked at each other with matching speculating facial expressions.

"So, what about the car? The drugs, guns, and money? Was that worth killing for? Rumor is that the trunk of that car was filled with bricks of cocaine and money."

"Well, maybe you should go find da car, ask da car, and leave me da fuck alone. I told you, I don't know shit!"

Swop! This time it was a back hand swing. I think I tasted blood in my mouth, salty and murderous. Yeah, it was blood. "Listen here you piece of shit. I'm going to send you back to that sewage hole that you dumb fucks call home. But before I do, let me warn you of a couple of things that may convince you to change your mind before you walk out of this building. One, if you try to tell anyone about what happened here, they wouldn't believe you anyway. So, that would be a waste of time. But hey, you're a real nigger anyway right? You guys don't break the codes of the streets." Graham was a funny ass nigga. For some reason, him calling me a nigger stung more than the couple of slaps to the face he gave me. I don't know why though. I and my niggas called each other niggas all the time. I guess the intent was different.

"Two," Graham continued, "right after we picked you up, I sent a few cars full of police officers to the same spot we got you from. Hopefully, your peers are dumb enough to assume that they showed up because of something you told us. So, whether you told me or not, I already had plans of letting you walk. If I were you, I'd grab the Draco before showing your face again."

"And finally, he stayed solid the first go around, but I'll get Anderson to talk. And when I do, you better pray that he doesn't mention your name. Not even a syllable." I wasn't worried about any of this shit this fool was talking about. Niggas know I'm stamped in my hood. I ain't telling shit about nobody opps included, and this nigga had another thing coming if he thought he was gone get Flex to tell some. I doubt if he even would be able to catch Flex alive without help from the military. My nigga done got on some other shit lately. Terrorizing terminator type shit.

" Well, baby dick, if that's all, I'd like to go now."

"As a matter of fact, Mr. Hawkins, actually that's not it." Black took charge. "When you go back out there, I want you to keep in mind that we have proof of your location on a murder scene that we expect to be our precinct snitch, telling Tim. Also, know that the investigation is ongoing and that one day, we just may be able to swap out a favor for a favor."

Fuck! Q said that the mistake of me taking my phone on that kill would come back to haunt me. I ain't really think too much about it back then. But I wished my nigga was here now. It seemed like he always knew what to do when it came to long-term situations.

"How about this?" Graham got back to wagging his shitty ass tongue. "We'll clear you on all future charges if you just admit right now that Ghost, DeQuan 'Q' Anderson, was the trigger man."

Why the fuck would they want to put the murder on Q? That was the dumbest shit I've ever heard a detective say. That might be a smart thing to do on my end though. I mean Q was dead right? Would I be wrong for making a dead man take his own spill? I mean what would they do? Lock his corpse up in a box for the rest of his breathless life. Even though I don't think that the ghost of Q would mind, I won't tell anybody even if it was a body.

"Listen," I made sure that I made eye contact with them both, "I said ion shit and that's what I meant. I ain't snitchin' on a soul. Not even a dead one." They gave each other that look again.

Graham chuckled. "Yo dumb ass really don't know shit huh?"

"What do you mean by that?"

"If you thought that Ghost was dead, then you are a fool."

"Guess it's true what they say huh?" Black jokes, "Ghosts really don't die."

All that symbolic spiritualism shit went over my head. I was ready to get the fuck out of here.

Scene 2: The Carter-Ward Kick Back Spot

I realized the water was deep, I thought. A part of me wanted to keep the rest of these niggas in the blind and allow me a better chance at getting ahead. But this war was them vs us. So, wisely, I had to put the gang on the game. I was already ringing Blu's line. Because I thought he would answer, I was half a second away from hanging up. Right before I did, he answered. "Hello."

"Yo, where the niggas at?"

"Kick Back."

"Who wit you?"

"I'm dolo." Silence followed. "Listen my nigga, des people are playin' chess wit our ass while we just dey here jumpin' pieces and shit. Dis shit ain't gone go on fo 'ever. Niggas need to get together and find a way to outthink these people. Da shit we do is crash dummy shit. I'm starting to think that this is exactly wat they want from us."

"Ight. Ight. Ight. Say no more dick. Stay where you at. Ima check with the niggas and we gone pull up."

Self Made Tay

Chapter 19: Flex's Frenzy
Scene: O-Block

"Who was dat?" I asked Blu as soon as he disconnected the call.
"Dat was Hawk."
"I told ya'll dat nigga said some! Wat's da coincidence of all dis shit happening in dis order. Dey pick him up, he gave da drop, and now his ass back on da streets dat fast? Now Lil Mark laying out der dead!" Blu nor Reggie had a word to say. What could they say? If I was tripping, will a nigga please shut me up?

"Brah say he in da kick back spot right no waitin' fo niggas to pull up. Say he needs to holla at niggas." I was surprised at the news Blu had just released.

"Oh, dis shit gone be easy. Call everybody up. Make sure dat no-fly zone is secured and tell niggas to meet us at da kick back. We bout to have us another 'Tellin' Tim Execution'."

Scene 2: The Kickback Spot

Everybody that needed to be here was present. Reggie and his two youngins, Boss Baby and Big Baby. Of course, Hawk was the reason for this gathering. Blu, Red, and a few other members stood by in preparation to watch their HNIC go down. Big Dee pulled up on behalf of the Bottom Boys. He decided to pull his right-hand man Real into the equation. Real had an undeniable intuition when a nigga was being real or flaw right off the back. He never missed his judgment. Burga was here as well. Ducked off to the side as usual.

Anyway, I came here to conduct a murder in a business manner. But first, I wanted to know exactly what it was that Hawk had to say. It was quiet and the silence was irking my nerves.
"Hawk," I spoke.
"Flex."
"Well, nigga, speak."
"I know dis may sound crazy, but I promise you, I can't make dis shit up. Dem people trying to set our ass up and play us against

each other. Dat nigga Graham told me to my face dat he sent 12 at ya'll to make it look like I was telling. But I swear, I ain't tell em shit. Dey ain't even have none on me to pick me up fo. Other than a bunch of hearsay. Dey threatened me wit Tim's murder and tried to get me to put it on Q."

"Hold up!" I interrupted. Hawk had me slightly convinced up until this point. I was familiar with the divide and conquer method. That was the whole purpose of them giving you the drugs, them the money, and a nigga like me the guns. So, that I could rob ya'll niggas for what I needed. You can sell them slow-killing poison for what they needed. And we both could make victims out of the niggas with the money. Code name crabs in a barrel. Also known as the Box. Best known "as the Projects.

But the mention of 12 wanting to put the charge off on Q threw me way left. "Why da fuck would dey try to get you to put the body on Q?" I pressed.

"Ion know. Dat's da same shit I asked dem niggas. Dey were talkin' some wild shit like Q wasn't dead or some … Like he was here in ghost form or sum shit."

"Naw, Q is definitely dead." The words arrogantly slipped out of my mouth. As soon as they did, I wished I could take them back. Since I couldn't, I was hoping that they flew over niggas heads. However, Reggie eyed me from his peripheral. I knew that he caught onto something, but that would be easy to clean up.

"What do you mean?" Reggie asked.

"What do you mean, what I mean?" I answered a question with a question.

"You just said dat Q was definitely dead. Like you knew for certain. Like you made sure of it or some."

"Reggie! Wat da fuck are you talkin' bout? We all know Q is dead. Ya'll were da ones dat called me and said ya'll have seen it fo yourself." That silenced Reggie but I could tell that he was still speculating.

"Anyway," I resumed, "what else dem pigs say?"

"Shit for real!" Hawk replied. "Dey were jus tryin' to figure out who Q was beefin' wit. Tryin' to find a suspect to pinpoint his murder on. Dey said something about a car he had full of bricks and money." I took a quick side look over at Reggie and could feel the heavy vibrations from his thoughts radiating off his brain. "But fuck all dat, cuz dem bitches don't know shit and wasn't talkin' bout shit. Dey jus fishing but Ima shark. Ion do no talkin' to da law. So, all ya'll niggas can miss me with dat shit. But wat's up with you though?" Everybody looked around the room at each other trying to figure out who Hawk was talking to. "You nigga!" He stared directly at me.

"Who?" I was honestly lost.

"You!! Don't try and play dumb. You all down my neck bout what happened when you talked to dem people. Why you ain't put niggas on game bout dat?" I was confused by Hawk's outburst and by the looks on their faces. So was everyone else. Some were even surprised.

"Ion know wat da fuck you talkin' about. I ain't do no talkin' to dem people. Matter of fact, I ain't even doin' no talking. I'm trying to kill every one of dem bitches I see out cha." I was growing hot at the fact that I had to stand here and defend my silence.

"Well, dat ain't what Graham said."

"So, what, are you callin' me a snitch?" I was six centimeters away from clutching my pistol depending on his response.

"Naw, I ain't sayin' dat. Come to think about it, da black cracker kept it real and said you ain't fold but gave me heads up dat he'll be back fo you." This confusion was now disturbing my composure. I thought I was the king of mind games. Now I wasn't sure if Graham had brain fucked Hawk, or Hawk was brain fucking me. Either way it went, I didn't want anything to do with this mental orgy. Pause.

"Maine, did nigga bullshitting." I snatched my pistol from under my Gucci belt buckle and gripped it tightly by my side, waiting for a nigga to attempt the draw. "I smell a rat!"

"Nigga, you got me fucked up!" Hawk stepped towards me as if I wasn't a deadly nigga holding a loaded gun. The dude was brave. At least I know that he was willing to die about this shit.

"You da one trying to hide shit. Why da fuck you just don't let niggas know what went down?"

I'm glad he was close enough. I grabbed Hawk by the collar of his shirt, pulled him closer to me, and raised the Glock to his face. "Ima say dis shit one more matha fuckin' time. I ain't talk to no pigs bout shit. You hear me? And if you or any other nigga ever say dat shit out ya mouth again…" It took everything in me not to let my gun finish off this sentence.

"Ayee Flex, chill brah. Dat nigga is really telling da truth. Real was approaching my side. I was ready to ask him how da fuck did he know. But like I said, he always knew.

"Yeah for real though. Ya'll niggas are tripping." Now Burga was spending his two cents, but I wasn't burying it. "Put dat ma'fuckin gun out dat Maine face. We are all on da same team. Dem people are trying to take ya'll out by putting ya'll against each other." Burga had gone and reached for the gun but before he could get his hand on it, I pulled it back. Nigga wasn't getting this bitch out of my hands.

"Ight brah," I gave in for now. "But I ain't jus gone let no nigga throw no bad bone on my name. Dats dead.

"Da man said, 'he stayed solid the first go-round but I'll get Anderson to talk.' It's only two Andersons I know out dis bitch. Dat's you and yo bro.. th..er."

Ok, now I was on fire. This nigga just keeps on insinuating that Q was alive. Just the thought of that being true was turning my stomach upside down. I was fiending and wanted to kill somebody to satisfy my high. Fuck a limb. Hawk was not the type of person that you could shoot and let live. So, I did what I do best, I aimed high and squeezed the trigger twice at rapid speed.

To my surprise, Burga rushed in front of the gun while grabbing it with both hands at the same time. The first shot had just missed his head. By the time the second one was exiting the chamber, I was subconsciously trying to regain control of the pistol.

The second Bow! From the sound effect of the gun silenced the entire apartment, bringing order out of all the chaos. Everybody stood still, stuck, staring at me. Including Burga. That was until he slopped forward towards me until his knees met the tile on the floor. With both hands, he still held a light grip on the gun. I had yet to release the grip of my own from the handle. I don't know where it came from, but I felt a tear sneaking from my left eye and creeping down my face. I watched a tear of blood crawl from inside Burga's body through the hole directly in the middle of his head. He fell backwards and as he did, the gun slid out of his hands. Once that happened, the weight of his body was shifted to the side. His body continued in that motion until it came into contact with the floor causing a loud thud to sound off. Burga was gone. Another fallen soldier.

I have never in my life been in an accidental murder, until today. There was no way for me to cover this one up. We all saw it. But they know I didn't mean to kill Burga. Matter of fact, I didn't kill Burga. He chose to make a sacrifice to save Hawk. That would be the story I painted in everyone's head, including my own.

"Look wat da fuck you did!" Hawk snapped. "You walkin' round dis bitch on yo high horse all in yo fuckin feelings. Now you have fuckin killed out nigga! All I was trying to do was put yo dumb ass on game bout dis knee-deep pile of shit dat you and yo brotha got us in and you wanna act like a fuckin homo thug."

"From dis point on Flex, Ion give a fuck wat you do. Just leave me da fuck out of it. And if any of ya'll fuckin wit dis psychopath, stay far away from me."

"But I..." I tried to speak but nothing would come together. "..I.. But...I." I'm glad no one had tried to kill me for this mistake I had just made. Gun still in hand, I slowly backed my way out of the apartment. On my way out, I was still fumbling with my words speaking in tongues. I needed a place to get myself back together.

Chapter 20: Q's Queries
Scene: Richmond City Jail Infirmary

"Are you ready?" A familiar voice questioned me.

"Wat?" was my reply.

"Are you ready?"

"Ready for wat?" Silence, but somehow that silence said a lot and it made a lot of sense. That's when I noticed that I was on a mountain-like hilltop. The mountain was filled with beautiful, healthy, green grass. The best I've ever seen. I was surrounded by a spacious, strong, and splendid forest of trees. They were occupied by exotic animals who ate, played, and rested. The sky seemed to be low, so low that if my arms were long enough, I could reach up and touch a cloud. These types of clouds didn't look like the type that held the purpose of storing water preparing the earth for rain. Instead, it looked as if they were there for decoration reasons only. The sky wasn't blue by the way, instead, it resembled a large rainbow of colors in no certain order. Purple here, orange there, spots of blue, explosions of red. It was like the famous painter Van Gough had blessed the sky with his famous strokes in an abstract manner.

Observing my surroundings placed me in a state of peace and tranquility. Yet, it didn't clarify my confusion. I looked directly in front of me and was faced with more confusion. I blinked my eyes twice in an attempt to make some sense out of my vision. Still completely baffled, I squinted my eyes attempting to channel my sight. What or who I saw was real. It was not an illusion. "Pops?"

"Son." I ran up to my Pops and wrapped both of my arms around him.

"I missed you so much," I expressed like the very little boy that he had left behind.

"Son, you were never without me. I was always with you. I will always be here for you." I noticed that he never returned my embrace. Instead, he placed both of his hands on each side of my shoulders and separated us far enough for us to embrace eye contact. "Are you ready son?" He asked me again although very patiently.

Without expression with my voice, I tried to figure out in my thoughts exactly what my Pops was getting at. Turns out, I didn't have to utter a word for him to detect my misunderstanding. "Son, you have a mission in your physical life that has to be fulfilled. And whether you are ready or not, opportunities are going to be presented to you. Whenever you are faced with doubt, bury it under faith and know that your fate will pave the way to success for you. Everything you've been through has prepared you for the next upcoming events in your life. If you are not ready, you need to be ready. You do not have time to get ready. Let's give thanks to our wonderful God for allowing me to meet you with this message."

"Pops took two steps backwards that landed him on a large stream of liquid that resembled a separate mixture of milk and honey. Oddly, he didn't sink into the liquid but rolled down the stream like he was on a hoverboard draped in his white and gold garments. "Pop! Wait, where you goin'? Don't leave me again!" I yelled.

"You were never without me son." He repeated with a shining bright smile on his face. I tried to travel on the river by standing on it the way my Pops did. Expectantly, I dropped underneath the bottomless existence of the substance. I was trying to find my way back to the surface as the liquid filled my body with an indescribable taste. It filled me with a sense of pleasure while killing me at the same time or was it giving me life?

I gasped for a deep breath of air as I sat up on my bunk, still in jail. I swear on everything, that dream felt as real as this waking moment. It seemed as if my life was unreal, or maybe that my real life was fake. I swear I either was getting smarter or crazier. My mind was becoming awakened to things that I didn't realize before. Like the signs on the TV. The messages in the books. The codes in the lyrics of a song. The symbols and logos represented around the world. I was now confused as to what was a lie and what was true.

As long as I've been here, I've had plenty of time to dump through most of the books here. I even read a few of them twice. I watched so much TV that I had begun to talk to it. Most of the time, I knew what it was going to say before it did. I meditated so much that I was barely here. I would wander off into past or future events. Other times, I would simply enjoy the moment of now, even though now may have been lonely and quiet. I'm talking about being so lonely that I would have hour-long conversations with myself. And, yes, I'm talking about the type of conversations where I answer my own questions. If it wasn't for the volume of the TV or the sound of slamming doors, I probably would have gone crazy due to the silence.

Chapter 21: Keyshia Keeps It Moving
Scene: Her New Residence

Today was finally the day I would be able to leave this project life behind me. In my hand, I held the keys to my new home. It was a few stars of luxury above my prior residence. The funny thing was that I was only a few minutes and a couple of turns away from Jackson Ward. Despite the short distance in travel, this whole new environment seemed like a whole new world. Surrounded by community security gates, I felt safe to be in a place where the gangsters couldn't play.

Strongly, this transition felt like a bittersweet one. I had so many memories in that last apartment with Q that it was almost hard for me to tear myself apart from it. I remember it like it was yesterday. Us walking through the door of that very same apartment. It makes it even worse that the last place he sat was beside me on the very same couch that we had bought.

Q always had dreams of moving our family out of the projects. He never knew exactly how he would do it but was certain that he would get it done. As the years went by, he seemed to become comfortable with living in the same projects that we grew up in. With that, I had begun to pile up a sense of doubt in my mind about his conception. That caused me to work a little bit harder because I refused to provide my daughters with the same lifestyle as my experience. Turns out that I was wrong and was woman enough to admit it. The wound from the cut was deep because he had actually got it done but was not here to feel the joy of his accomplishments. To see the smiles on his daughters' faces. So, I could tell him how happy and proud I was for him. This made me feel like shit, even though I no longer lived in a dump.

"Mommy, dis our new house?" The youngest of my two daughters had asked full of enthusiasm. We were pulling up to our new domain.

"Yes Demia. This is our new house."

"It's pretty."

"It's clean too." DeAsia chimed in. "Is daddy coming to sleep with us?" DeAsian and Demia had yet to grasp the concept of the absence of their father. It kind of made it hard without the ritual of a funeral. The last thing they remember of their father was them three laughing and playing together. That was only moments before his death. I swear I tried to hide my hurt and be as strong as I could for them. But unintentionally, they made it seem almost impossible.

Chapter 22: Q's Qualms
Scene: Richmond City Jail Infirmary

All day long, I've been contemplating on the illustration of my dream from last night. It left me in a state of extreme anxiety. I felt as if I was surrounded by people that weren't here. Like I was being surveillance by someone other than the people watching the cameras. In addition to all that paranormal shit, I was racking my brain trying to understand the words of my Pops. What was he talking about? How could I be ready for something that I knew nothing about? I spent each passing second in anticipation of something magically spiritual happening. Instead, all I witnessed was a deep silence.

Strongly, I began to focus on that silence. As soon as I thought I was able to make something out of the nothingness of absent sound, the door was loudly buzzing open. Two COs walked through the door. One barring a pair of handcuffs. Followed by their entrance, the door was slammed shut three times louder than the buzz that unlocked it. With the combination of stomping boots, dangling keys, clicking cuffs, and other very annoying sounds, I was already beginning to miss the soundlessness of the same silence that damn near drove me crazy from its misunderstanding.

"Anderson, time to take a trip." It was transportation. Don't ask me where I was going because I was clueless my damn self. In my situation, one would expect it to be a court, right? Right, I was thinking and hoping the same thing. However, the strange thing was that out of all this time I spent here, I had yet to have a court appearance. Nor a visit from a lawyer to represent me. I didn't even know exactly what charges I was facing. Guess I'll find out today.

The links on the shackles were few. They damn near took my legs away from me. I was forced to take slow and steady steps. I was handcuffed to the extreme so much so that they even wrapped a chain around my waist. This was definitely physical evidence of modern-day slavery. The cuffs around my wrist itched and irritated the very same scar that was placed there by another set of cuffs by that asshole Detective Graham. Would you believe that I had to pluck and pull my own stitches out?

Eventually, we were in the van. I was in the back of course. We were parked in the garage of the jail. As we sat there, I mentally questioned why the fuck was I alone. How did I earn the privilege of ducking the long process of a packed bullpen, awaiting a ride? The door was yanked open. One of the two COs that chained me up, tossed an all-black miniature pillowcase-like fabric on my lap. "Put dis on." He ordered.

I just stared at him. For one, what he thought I was stupid. For two, I was trying to see if his ass was stupid. Must be. I couldn't put that shit on my head even if I wanted to. Hell, I couldn't even reach up to scratch the itch on my nose. Which I definitely wanted to do. He stepped up in the van and grabbed the pillowcase. "You know you're going to have to learn how to cooperate if you want to make this process easy." Talking about shit being easy. Ain't shit in my life been easy. I ain't say shit. But in my head, I assured myself that I would never in my life cooperate with the police. Not the fake police, real police, Black police, or White. He pulled the cover over my head, exited the van, and slammed the door.

Sitting in the pitch-black pillowcase, I heard the garage door draw open. The van pulled off slowly. My heart began to race at a fast pace. I don't know why it took so long for me to realize this, but it did. Something abnormal was behind this extradite. This was far from normal court procedure. This was a kidnap.

With my sight eliminated, the only sense of direction I had was the motion of the car. I thought I would be able to catch certain sounds to help paint a better picture. But the CO wisely blasted the radio so that it was all I heard. They were Black, so Polo G and Lil TJay's 'Popout' was the current song. This was actually my first time hearing the song, but I immediately fell in love with it. The van swayed around the horseshoe-like curve, exiting the garage. That part was easy and so was the next. Speed bump, then we were picking up speed through the lengthy parking lot. After a quick pause, swerve right and I knew we were heading up the hill on Fairfield Way. Obviously, it was a red light because we stopped at the intersection at the top of the hill. A little less than a minute later, the gas was pushing the van in motion again. The steering wheel directed it to make a left on Mechanicsville Turnpike. We picked up speed continuing in a straight direction.

Another intersection, another stop which I concluded to be another red light. I knew these streets of Richmond better than I knew the lines in the palm of my own hand. I knew exactly where we were. To the right were a gas station and the community grocery store. To the left were 360 Convenient Store and Whitcomb Court Projects. If we proceeded straight, however, we would be entering the city limits that were boarded by Henrico County and further than that was Hanover County. Either way, it was opposite of the route to the John Marshall Courthouse.

I found out a few moments later that neither option was the premeditated route. Instead, after going through the lights, the van veered right hopping on the ramp to the highway. I knew this entrance was eastbound. From there, I was afraid that I would get lost in the speed of the travel. Then there was hope. The ride was so fast that it made the distance shorter than I remembered. There were only a few exits in between the distance from the sharp upward slope followed by a soft hook at the top along with a quick pump of the brakes at the stop sign. I knew it was the Nine Mile exit.

The driver made a right. Why Creighton? I wondered. We were literally on the strip of the projects. I guess thinking that he had all the sense, the driver made a u-turn almost immediately. If his attempt was to throw my sense of direction off, it was to no avail. We rode up Nine Mile Road into the Henrico area and now I could safely say that I was lost. There were just too many intersections. Too many options to stop at. I had an idea, but no definite location. Eventually, we made a right and slowed down. 21 Savage and J. Cole's 'A lot' was the music to my ear that kept me composed. The next thing I knew, the radio was being shut off. The van came to a stop. I heard a speaker box come on. Something like a drive-thru restaurant. "From where?" Was all the voice of the lady asked?

"Jeremiah 13." The CO replied. I then heard gates retracting open. For the first time on this trip, the driver drove like he had some sense down an elongated driveway. Soon, we were going around a roundabout. After almost a third of the distance around the big circle, we parked at the halfway mark. The driver's door opens. Passenger door followed. They both slammed at damn near the same time making it hard to tell who was first. Seconds later, the back door of the van was being piled open.

My heart was beating at a racing pace. I'm not sure if I could say that I was scared. Because to be honest, I don't think I was. I was anxious to know where I was. Why was I here? A foot stepped into the van. I guess I may be finding out soon. A hand grabbed me by the arm and yanked me out of the seat. Feet grounded on the surface of the earth, I tried to get a feel for the texture laying under my feet. It was like stone. I wasn't able to play that game for too long. My law protecting kidnappers were guiding me to .... A step. And a few more after that. I counted 12. A few steps later, I was forced to stop. Another buzz followed by what sounded like a whole different voice out of another speaker box. "From where?"

"Jerimiah 13." The CO replied with the same answer to the same question asked only a couple of New York minutes ago.

"Invited by?"The voice vibrating out of the speaker box wanted to know.

"Supreme. The GrandMaster."

"You came to?"

"Contain the one who lives to edge God out." The door buzzed open. From the freshness, breeze, and smell of the air, I knew that this was not another jail. We walked through the door and slowly glided down a corridor. You know the thing that was now starting to spook me out at least a little, was the fact that neither one of these fuckers said a word to me or each other. I was starting to conclude that they were more than just jail COs. They were acting more like Secret Service agents. Maybe I was going to meet the President. Hope it's for a pardon.

We came to another door with another line of questions before being allowed to enter.

"From where?"

"Jerimiah 13."

"Invited by?"

"Supreme. The GrandMaster."

"You came to?"

"Contain the one who lives to edge God out."

"Who is God?" I realized that with every level advanced, there were a couple more questions tacked on.

"The one and only Great Architect of the Universe."

"What is the job of the Universe?"

"To create and apply the laws of the Great Architect."

"How?"

"As within. So, without. As above, so below."

"Password?"

"To be at one with self is to be at one with God."

Buzz....

Self Made Tay

Chapter 23: Flex's Frailties
Scene: Ducked Off

I'm ducked off in a telly. I really didn't want anyone to know where. So, I can't tell you. But I did tell one person. Seems like the only person I could trust right now. You might remember the bitch even though I never dropped her name. Glad I didn't because it was that little police bitch.. Shawty has been really loyal. I mean she knew exactly what was going on. Shit, she knew a lot. She kept it all between us. In addition to that, she'd tip me off with certain tips on their moves and plans.

Right now, I felt like I really needed a companion. Lil' Mark went out in a blaze of glory because of me and Burga just died. Even though I didn't mean to, it was by my hands. I'm pretty sure the whole hood was against me right now. I'm also starting to have small doubts about Q being dead. As I look back at the recent events and actually listen to the words spoken, two and two just weren't adding up. Of course, I've tried to get Lil' Shawty on top of that. For some reason, she claimed that she couldn't get any information on DeQuan Anderson.

"You need to get yo rank up." I encouragingly teased.

"Boy, fuck you. I ain't trying to be no super cop. You gotta do all dat extra-ass police shit. Besides, I ain't even want to be dis anyway."

"So, why da fuck are you doin' it?" I took a hit from the blunt I had just rolled and sparked.

"It's kind of like my father made me do it because he was this big detective." Detective, I thought in my head. She rambled on. "Actually, he was groomin' my big brother to be dis super cop. But he was killed in a high-speed chase. Next thing I knew, it seemed like all the pressure was on me to follow in my father's footsteps."

"Why didn't you just say dat you ain't wanna do dat shit?"

"Because my father provides me wit everything, and he is big on wat he calls carrying da legacy of da Grahams in law enforcement." I definitely caught that one. This bitch just said Graham.

After saying that her father was a detective, I never knew her last name. I guess I know now. These two and two were definitely adding up. For now, I made a quick decision to play dumb as to what I just heard. I wasn't completely sure if this bitch was really for me or just trying to set me up. Either way, I had plans on finding out for sure.

"Look, long as you fuckin' wit me, you don't have to worry about shit. If you got me like you really say you do, den I definitely got you."

"I hate when my loyalty is questioned."

"I didn't question your loyalty."

"You said if. Placin' doubt in yo belief. When I say I'm wit you, den dat's wat it is. Haven't I shown you dat by now?"

"Yeah, but maybe you gone have to keep showin' me."

"Oh, yeah?" was all she said. "How do you want me to show you? Like dis?" She went down on me and filled her mouth up with my dick. I moaned a little as thoughts traveled through my brain.

"Dis is definitely a good start, but I got some other shit in mind on top of dat." She tried to lift her head up to say something but I grabbed the back of it and forced her to stay down before she could get up. "Now, don't stop, just listen. I got a nice lil stash put up. I'm only willin' to spend it if it makes me more money. I think I have a way of upgradin' our status to business partners." She tried to bring her head up for air. I pushed it back down on the dick again.

"I need you to find more officers like you. Ma'fuckas dat's just out 'cha tryna get paid. Dat really can give .. AAahh... two fucks bout makin' da world a better place. We're gonna make you captain. You know something like startin' our own society. You gone handle all yo bad cops. Dat means payments, information, and even clipping whoever gets weak along da way." I could tell that she was feeling the plan. The more I explained, the better she mopped the dick up.

"Umm.. Trust me. Together you and I will have da city eatin' out of our hands."

Chapter 25: Q's Questions
Scene: Who Fucking Knows?

The least I knew was that we stepped into a room and the door closed behind us. Soon I found out that we were facing someone. This time the voice was in person. No speaker box. "From where?" a man asked.

"Jeremiah 13."

"Invited by?"

"Supreme. The GrandMaster."

"You came to?"

"Contain the one who lives to edge God out."

"Who is God?"

"The one and only Great Architect of the Universe."

"What's the job of the universe?"

"To create and apply the laws of the one and only Great Architect."

"How?"

"As within, so without. As above, so below."

"Password?"

"To be at one with self is to be at one with God."

"Please present a sign." I could tell that movement was being made out of course. I couldn't see anything.

"Please remove the veil from Jerimiah 13." I wasn't sure who Jerimiah 13 was, but I was once again grateful to have my sight back. And boy, it was a sight to see. It was a foyer. Some type of lobby. It looked like the inside of a mansion, with some of the best materials used to decorate the interior. Marble floors, a winding staircase with a pearl railing. The ceiling was high. I mean high, high, and obtained to hold what seemed like the only window in the building so far. That window held paintings of multiple spiritual figures. Also from the ceiling, hung a chandelier with no lights. Yet it still shined with a mixture of crystals and diamonds. Attached to the ceiling as well were two great pillars. Of course, they both dropped, finding their way to the floor. One was way left, and the other was far off to the right. I looked around in admiration. I wondered what I owe to be blessed enough to take in this beautiful sight.

"Jerimiah 13, welcome my long-lost child." I focused my attention directly in front of me and was face to face with … I don't know who the fuck the dude was. I was still coming up short as to who the fuck Jeremiah 13 was. With that, I just stared at the dude. He dressed kind of weirdly. The weirdest thing was that his attire almost resembled the same thing that my Pops wore in the dream he visited me in. Sticking to my old techniques, I said nothing. Just waited for my questions to be answered.

"I am delighted to accept you into our first class of the 2021 Lost Cultivation Society." What? I only asked in my mind. "We have waited a very long time for your grateful entrance. I am sure that you are unaware, but our membership is predestined due to specific bloodlines. Here, we teach you the secret to true abundance of wealth, health, and prosperity. Even a fool has the ability to generate money, but only a wise man can reserve or multiply his money."

"Very soon you will have a very great decision to decide on. Your choice will dictate your near and far future. A very grand gift in joining this Brotherhood is unlimited potential. Have we not removed you from the internal pains of a slaved jail cell into the luxurious halls of our beautiful, peaceful lodge? Yet, that is nothing compared to the unknown forces of Heaven and hell that will bring great life-changing events. At the end, the choice is all yours. We as a people are just fulfilling our obligations to our brother. Before we proceed, I humbly warn you to choose with extreme caution for we here are bonded by secrecy. We vow to never let a weak leak spill our secrets to the unworthy." Did this nigga just threaten me? Reading between the lines, that's definitely what it sounded like.

"Do you have competent understanding?" The man draped in all white asked me. I simply nodded with a yes. He made a gesture with his right hand and just like that, the COs, or whatever they were, were uncuffing me from all the chains that had my body captive. To be honest, I was confused. The feeling of freedom overrode my confusion though. With a waving motion, the COs followed behind the man. On my own will, I did as well. I wasn't sure if it was due to curiosity or the fact that it seemed like I had nothing to lose. I just hoped that my nosiness didn't get me killed. Either way, it went from this point. I guess I'll be taking this one to the grave for sure.

Chapter 26: Flex's Forsaken Ego
Scene: Ducked Off Still

After I sent Lil Shawty on her mission, I sat melancholy alone trying to come up with a plan of my own. For the life of me, I could not put together how Q was able to live surrounded by so much wickedness and still rule with honor. If I could, I'd dig his grave up, take some advice, and put his ass back in the mud. "You're a stupid matha fucka 1." I could have sworn I heard somebody say. I was certain that I was the only one in this room. I had grown so mentally unstable that I made sure I searched this bitch every thirty minutes or so. "You think you are me, but you are not."

"I know I ain't tripping." I grabbed my gun off the stand. "Who da fuck is dat?" I felt stupid for asking that question.

"It's me. Your ego."

"My ego? Nigga, what da fuck are you talking about? I am my ego!" Now I know I wasn't tripping. I actually could hear this fucking voice talking to me. It was in my head, or was my mind playing tricks on me?

"You don't even know wat you're doing. You are just doing shit. In da matha fuckin way. Talkin bout you a King!" Nigga, you ain't no fuckin King! What type of King divides and kills their own people? Even the worst King knows that is stupid."

"Nigga, fuck you!" I was getting pissed. At nothing. "I ain't mean to do dat shit!" I defended myself.

"Oh, but you did. It was all yo fault. Everything is yo fault. You are a fuck up. Oh, but don't trip doe. Dats wat you were made to do. Fuck shit up! The question is, wat you gonna do now? Wat do you plan to fuck up next?"

"Maine, shut da fuck up. I got dis shit nigga. You know who da fuck I am?"

"You can't shut me up. You made me. So, yeah, I know exactly who you are. It's just dat from ova here, I can see things a little clearer." I shot my eyes across the room. No one was there. "You let your emotions cloud your judgment."

"Shidd .. Nigga, ain't shit soft bout me."

"Yo emotion enemy is anger. You think you can do everything on your own. So ignorant dat you don't even know how to use da people around you."

"If you don't shut da fuck up!" I placed the gun up to my temple. "I will blow your fuckin brains out!"

"You might as well. You yo worst enemy anyway. You yo real opp. Ha.." the voice even laughed at me. "And even then, you won't be able to shut me up. You have to live with me through life and death." Sitting in a chair, I looked ahead of me and stared into a mirror. "I advise you to let me live though. Plus, I don't think you should really do dat. Ain't no coming back from dat. I'm pretty sure da devil has plans for you when you get to hell. Wat he's capable of doing is a thousand times worse than wat I can do to you."

"Nigga, fuck you nigga! I am da devil." Bow!

Chapter 27: Q's Answers Written in Blood
Scene: N/A

They were maple wooden double doors with trims and carvings of gold. Who I knew as Supreme, The GrandMaster knocked twice. Paused. Knock three times, and then twice more. Both knobs were turning from the inside. The doors were open, and we stepped through.

A long table sat in the middle of the room. All the chairs were in use by someone except the two at each end. The people in the chairs were covered in all-black hooded robes. "The Grand Master welcomes Jeremiah 13," Supreme announced. Everyone with their heads down and covered at the table raised a right hand. Never looking up, I started to clearly understand now that I had to be Jeremiah 13. I wasn't tripping though. I liked the alias. Just another code name I could use. I ain't want these people to know my real name anyway. "Please take your seat Jeremiah 13," Supreme suggested. With that, the two men entered the room and stood on guard.

I slowly walked over to the empty seat and sat calmly. The first thing I noticed was that this was the most comfortable seat I have ever sat in. It was plush, yet sturdy. Felt like a throne made for a real king. I looked down at Supreme on the other end of the table. In front of him sat a gavel. This definitely wasn't a court-room. So, don't ask me why. Shit, this was my first time here just like you. Soon, I found out exactly why.

Supreme lifted the gavel in his right hand and tapped it heavily on the table once. "All hail to the summoned acclaimed." Every-one stood. I remained seated. The gavel was tapped once again. Everyone covered their heart with a hand sign that was unknown to me. Two more taps from the gavel and the hoods were being removed from heads. Revealing the hidden identities. Three more quick taps and everyone was seated again.

First of all, I noticed that the knocks on the door matched the taps on the tables. Which was a total of seven. Second of all, which is what I should have said first. "Wat..da..fuc- "

"Jeremiah 13, you are to guard your tongue in this presence." My jaw was left hanging after being cut off my sentence by a letter. My awareness was stunned as if I had been ambushed or something. I was in a state of astonishment. The surrealism seemed miraculous. I definitely didn't see this one coming.

Streets, knowledge, Mr. Carter, and a few of my old construction workers, Top Shoota, the nurse from the hospital, Shayemane, and even Detective Black, along with a nice list of other people whom I didn't know. They all stared back at me with blank faces. I couldn't read emotion on either one of them. I didn't even know what to say. I wasn't even sure if it was real. On the other hand, I couldn't deny the fact that I was just freed from a jail and dragged here. Not everything, but a lot of shit was definitely starting to make sense now.

"Jeremiah 13, we will now proceed with your summon." I was starting to think that no one was allowed to talk except Supreme. "We will commence your initiation. Depending on how hard you decide to work determines the amount of time it may take. The Power of the will is solely yours."

"You were committed through the blood of your father, who served as a sacrifice for you.." What? As if my mind wasn't already racing. "Therefore, there's no need for you to make any diabolical wages unless your wish is to exceed with expedience. Otherwise, you will be properly and cautiously guided by the people you see here. Some you know, and others not so much." Supreme, 'The GrandMaster' paused his .. 'summons.' No one said a word. Not even me. What the fuck was I supposed to say? It was so much. I could say a thousand words at one time.

"First, you have to seal the summon." A piece of paper was brung to me on a silver platter, literally. "And know that when called upon a favor, you are to fulfill your obligations. No exceptions." The doorman laid the platter on the table in front of me. The paper was a contract. I noticed there wasn't a pen.

"We can now present the illustration .. Jerimiah 12." Every eye in the room shifted to whoever I guess Jeremiah 12 was. So now my eyes were too. "You have been exempt through exile."

Two men that sat beside Jeremiah 12 quickly yanked him by his throat. Two other men pulled both of his arms behind his back. You could tell that they have done this plenty of times before. The doorman was now walking a bronze platter over to Jeremiah 12. There was a pair of silver scissors and a very distinguished-looking knife. One of the men that already had Jeremiah 12 yoked by the neck, used a hand to force his mouth open. The other man used a hand to grab the scissors. Somebody reached in his mouth to snatch the man's tongue out. With no hesitation, the scissor man maliciously cut off his tongue with a hatred snip. With the tongue in his hand, the other man stuffed it back into the mouth of Jeremiah 12. He kept his hand covered over his mouth, forcing him to keep it closed. Used his other hand to grab the knife and swiftly sliced it across Jeremiah 12's neck. Blood gushed from his neck like a pair of sprinklers just turned on. They removed him from the room through a door that I never even knew was there.

"Jeremiah 13." Supreme began speaking once more. "You may now stamp the seal of the summons." The doorman laid down a razor blade and a .. stamp maker.

I looked from the platter and stared at everybody watching me. I don't know what the fuck they expected me to do. I mean, I now figured that they wanted me to sign this contract in blood. But, I had no clue as to what I was signing my life over to.

Then it hit me. I didn't even have a life. For the past some odd months, I was basically nonexistent. What did I really have to lose? Exactly. I lost my brother to dishonor. Lost my life to my brother. Lost my freedom, family, and finances. One thing I did know now though, was that there was nothing lost that I couldn't get back.

I've seen the ghost of my soul. Visited my father in the land of gold. Watching my brother turn me cold. Afterwards, I had to sit for months in wonderment about it all. On top of this shit that I'm seeing right now, you couldn't tell me that anything was impossible.

I grabbed the razor and put a cut on my index finger. We all watched as I dripped the blood on the line of the contract and smeared it with the stamp. It turned out to be a symbol I'd never seen before. "With this, you are to conceal the secrets within the confinements of yourself. Nothing of what you see is to be spoken on." Of course, no one spoke but Supreme. But who was I to tell? Even if I did, no one would believe this bullshit anyway. "Can we please take Jeremiah 13 to be cleansed now?" The woman who I met as Nurse Porter assisted by the only other woman in the room was now ushering me out of the room.

Chapter 28: Flex's Flat
Scene: Highway

You know I had to get the fuck out from that other spot. I don't know why, but my dumb ass went and shot the mirror. I'm just so fucking mad. I'm even beefing with myself. I know for a fact that I'm not thinking clearly. I don't even give a fuck. I was on my way to somewhere else. The only thing was, I didn't know where to go. I mean duhh. I could go duck off in another hiding spot. But what the fuck was I running from? I realized that no matter where I went, I would find a way to cause some type of chaos. If I'm alone, then I'll cause it with myself. I might as well go and take it out on someone else. Besides, I basically started most of the shit that's going on. Why not finish it? I was doing the same thing I accused Q of doing. Trying to run off and shit. I ain't running from shit. That's my hood. Ain't nobody gonna tell me I can't pull up. Not the opps or the cops. I mean, yeah, Ima break the law like I was trying to make a change. Who's law was it anyway? If it's their law, then fuck the law!

Whoop! Just one. Ain't that some shit. Fuck! I looked down at the dashboard. 15 mph over the speed limit. Ok, that's cool. I can definitely work on this. Either that or I'm smashing the gas. Straight doing the race on their ass. Ima try my hand first though. I popped the glove compartment, dropped the gun inside, and searched for plan A. It was an id card. It was Q's. I had taken it out of that car along with everything else in that bitch before I trashed it. I figured it would come in handy. I wonder if it will work. I lifted the top to the armrest and pulled out plan B. A fresh stack of hundreds adding up to ten bands. If I had to pay my way through this maze, then fuck it, I will. Plan C was no plan at all. Simply life or death. You probably think I'm tripping huh? I got two pistols up front, two assault rifles in the trunk along with a brick of soft. I was supposed to chill, break it down, and get me some money. But ...

Anyway, I pulled over to the right shoulder of the highway. You know 12 did the same. "Turn the car off!" Hands on the wheel!" A voice dispatched. I turned the car off but kept the key in. Put my hands on both sides of the steering wheel and waited.

The plain-clothes policeman got out of his car and slammed the door. He was riding in a 1968 Mustang GT. The fastback joint. I ain't gonna lie, that joint was like that. Royal blue paint with bumble bee yellow trimmings. He walked up to my door, and I knew exactly who he was. It was Detective Black cracker jack ass. "Hey buddy." He paused, giving me a suspicious look. I'm pretty sure he knew who I was as well. In fact, I'm sure. "You know you were doing damn near over 20 mph right?" It was 15, but whatever.

"Sorry Officer. I didn't realize dat." I played dumb.

"Let me see some ID please." I handed it to him. He looked at it and looked at me with a look that was unexplainable right now. Remember when I told you I had two up front? Well, the second gun was on the side of the driver's door. I was already slowly sliding my hands down to the bottom of the wheel dropping them in my lap.

How was I supposed to know that out of all the crackers in the city, he would be the one to fall out of the box? One of my main thoughts was that this was the perfect chance to break this cracker. Another thought was how dumb I was to use Q's id period, especially during a traffic stop. How was I to explain that if they ran his name and it came up deceased? Oh yeah, I won't be giving out any explanations.

Detective Black frowned curiously for a few eerie seconds. I guess he was finally starting to find out who I was. "How?" he paused, looked at the ID and waved it. "You know what?" He rubbed his forehead with his pitched fingers. "It's been a long day and I just clocked out. Today you are very lucky." He handed me the ID back. "It's really not worth the paperwork. I definitely don't feel like going through the extra bullshit. Just slow the fuck down. You're making the highway hot." He walked off tapping the hood. "Nice car by the way."

I guess today was a lucky day for me. About time something good comes my way. I'm trying to figure out what was up with the dude though. He just gone let a nigga go like that. I told you they were overlooking the real predators. I should smoke his ass just for disrespecting me like that.

I took my time pulling off, letting Detective Black get a good distance between us. I was so fucked up in the head that I thought about following him and stalking his family. But right now, I have other shit to handle. I switched my route up and headed south on 95.

Picking up speed, I weaved through the light traffic. Have you ever felt like doing the dash and flipping the car? Those were the type of thoughts that traveled through my mind. I was on my way back around da ward. I don't know what the fuck I was going to do. I just knew I was going back.

Switching over lanes, something caught hold of my tire popping the air out of the rubber. The car fished-tailed a bit, but thankfully, I guess, I was able to withhold control of the steering wheel. Now where I was again, making my way over to the right shoulder of the road.

Self Made Tay

Chapter 29: Q In the Pleasure of Doom
Scene: Pleasure of Doom

I was escorted to a bathroom which was actually the side of a one-bedroom apartment. A full closet packed with all kinds of male designer clothing. The tub had a room to itself. I opted for the shower instead. It was made of glass and had a smokey like a steam room.

I stood alone in the midst of the pouring waters. In the mix of rinsing the soap off my body, and allowing the suds to carry the filth of my body down the drain, the foggy shower door opened. Just like I imagined, without that nurse uniform on, Shayemane's body was banging like hair covering the forehead. It looked as if her body was hand-crafted by the Almighty Creator Himself, making her resemble a Goddess. It seemed as if her skin glowed with a shine that made the fog lose its density. She wore gold bangles and ankle bracelets, finger and earrings, and gold finger and toenail polish. A gold ribbon that was tied into a perfect bow pulling her hair to the back in a ponytail. Even in her nakedness, everything on her still seemed to match.

Shayemane stepped into the shower with me and out of her shadow, appeared a second woman. She had this almost pitch-black skin tone that still glowed like neon lights. She was a little bit slimmer and taller than Shayemane. Her accessories were also up to par. Her cosmetic appearance was on point. The shape of her body curved like an hourglass. She was like the mother of endless age.

Now, both of these extremely beautiful women were stuffed in this steaming sweatbox with me. Butt ass naked. Shayemane circled around to the front of me and stood face to face. She grabbed me by the dick and gently massaged it. The Black Queen walked behind me and massaged the back of my shoulders. She kissed me on the nape of my neck and sucked on it. Shayemane used her free hand and grabbed my chin. She stuck her tongue so far in my mouth that I could taste the sweet drips of her saliva and feel it draining down my throat.

All that went through my mind were the thoughts of my dick. There were so many things I anticipated doing to these two, that I wanted to get to it right now. It seemed though that they had plans of their own. Shayemane dropped to her knees and used her tongue to play with my dick. I wanted so desperately for her to put it in her mouth. The dark goddess behind me rubbed my neck while still planting kisses. "A Taurus." She said. "And you are so sexy." Whispering in my ear. By now, I knew better than to wonder how she knew the horoscope of my birth. Aside from that, I thought back to the last time I felt a woman's touch in such a sensuous way. Come to think of it, the last time was when I got the head from Shayemane's championship top-giving ass.

Yelp, just how I remembered. The same as I had dreamed of and fanaticized during my so many months of solitude. Shayemane's mouth was just as wet and warm as I left it. Minus the anxiety, agitation, and pain from the hospital. Shayemane's head game was extended to a magnitude of greatness. It felt so good. It felt like. "Ahh …" It felt like heav …" Oooch! Bitch!" It felt like Heaven.

Shayemane stuffed as much of my dick in her mouth as she could fit, bit down on it while deep throating it, and shooked a locking shake on it. Like a pit bull, tugging on a teddy bear, the godmother behind me gave me a stinging slap to the side of my face. "Watch your mouth now." She said getting back to kissing and massaging my neck, shoulders and back. The head doctor. I mean the nurse was now juggling and massaging my balls with one of her freshly French-manicured hands. She slowly slid my dick out of her mouth and sucked on the tip of it. My dick was so hard, it felt like it was about to explode. As soon as I thought I was coming, she stopped, stood up and snatched me by the dick. "Follow me King." She seductively suggested.

I ain't really have a choice but to follow Shayemane. She yanked at my manhood while pulling me out of the shower. I succeeded in Shayemane's pursuit, and the shadow of Eve proceeded me. Through our transition, Shayemane's Assistant snatched up a towel at first, she used it to dry us off. Afterwards, she grabbed a black and golden robe with stripes like a tiger. The ladies remained naked. Thank God the walk was a short one. After biting, stopping my cum, yanking and pulling on my dick, I'm pretty sure I was well on my way to a sack of blue balls. Moving along. Through the bathroom and straight into the .. bedroom, but it wasn't a bedroom. It didn't even have a bed. Instead, ropes, grips, chains, swings, and all types of other shit hung down from the ceilings. Animals rugs, of lions, tigers, and bears with their heads still on them. I walked through to take in all and in a nice size closet was .. an empty floor. In that floor was a pit full of snakes. Above this pit were two sex swings hanging from a super extended ceiling. I definitely didn't have any plans of getting on that ride.

Chapter 30: Flex's Flexibilities
Scene: Highway

The car had a spare, but I didn't have the tools or experience to change it. Shouldn't be that hard? I could at least figure that out. I needed to get back on the road like right now. I really don't have time to wait on a tow truck or anything like that. But something had to give. I was on my phone scrolling for an option when I noticed a car pulling up behind me. It was a State Police patrol car. The trooper operating it was already exiting the vehicle.

Leaning on the driver's side of my car, I acted as if I didn't even notice the cop approaching my left side. "Excuse me sir. Is everything alright?" He asked me, moving with more caution with every step.

"Huh?" I acted surprised. "I didn't notice you there, officer. Yeah, everything is cool. Just caught a flat. Waiting for help to arrive."

"Ok. Is there anything that I may be able to help you with?"

"Naw. Like I said, everything is cool. Jus waitin.' Dey on da way."

"Do you need me to sit by and wait with you? Because I don't mind sir." You know what's crazy? Is that this nigga was pissing me off! This nigga was too nice. I don't know if he was faking or just green. But that nigga had the wrong script.

"Yes sir. I'm sure. Thank you." I continued to play along. "I really appreciate da concern. Hope you enjoy da rest of your day sir." So many times, I thought about cursing this pig out or even popping his top. At least until I remembered I had a flat. It burnt me up inside to even act grateful to this bitch ass nigga. I was trying to figure out how he was so cool with being willing to help without being hateful. What world was he living in? Did he not realize who the fuck I was? Good thing I had the ability to throw him off. Think this was a good time to not be bad. Besides, the dude seemed like one of the good ones. He really thought his position was set into place to bring peace to the world. I'm laughing.

"Ok sir, you have a nice day as well. I hope it gets better. I'm going to get back into traffic. You make sure you stay safe out here." He got into his car and pulled off into traffic just as he said he would, leaving me standing there to plot my next motive.

I watched as the patrol car disappeared from the sight of my vision. I stuck my thumb out hitching for a ride. Somebody was naïve enough to pull over a short distance in front of my parked car. They backed their car back into mine. Bag in my right hand, I hurried to the car. It was an old, small lady. Aww how nice of granny! Stupid bitch. I should carjack her ass, kidnap her, and hold her hostage in the back of the trunk. I ain't about to do all that right now. A nigga just needs a ride for real. Get the fuck off this highway.

Chapter 31: Q In the Pleasure of Doom Part II
Scene: Pleasure of Doom

It's so many women everywhere. All kinds, shades of race, shapes, and sizes. They were elaborate, eloquent, and excruciating. They were very pleasurable. Also, violently painful. They made me their sex slave. They tortured me. Threw me back into bondage by chaining me up forcefully. Beat the shit out of me with ropes and whips. Did damn near everything imaginable to my dick. Allowing me to experience some of the most extreme pleasures. But was punished purposely by not having the chance to bust a nut. Not once. They definitely did things that mesmerized the memories in my mind. Although it was as if they had a perfect timing of the ejaculation of my semen, they would erect it, await it in a pleasurable bliss and stop.

In between the pleasure and tease, the pain and torture, I had begun to develop a numbness to my feelings. I think it came from the confusion or realization of the concept of feeling. The agony and the feelings of pleasure brought misery and anxiety. It pained me that I couldn't obtain the thing that I desperately needed at this very moment. On the flip side of the coin, I had grown to endure the pain and actually found ease in the anticipation of the healing. Right now, I was hands tied behind my back, hanging upside down from the ceiling. Been like this for 30 minutes now. One of the exotic masterpieces unhatched a latch on the wall that sent me headfirst to the cushions of the floor. Two other dimes helped me up by my arms and sat me down on the floor. The blood in my body was in hot pursuit to the bottom half of my body. Moments later, two other women came from another area of the room carrying a rectangular floor table. It contained all types of foods from garlic, chaga, mushrooms, beets, and fruits like lemons, goji berries, watermelon, grapes, and bananas. Two more beauties came over. Both barring two different pitchers of liquids. One set of the two pitchers contained milk in one and honey in the other. These two again. The other set was both filled with ice-cold water. They fed me almost everything. Even when they had to force it, flooding my bladder with water, milk, and honey. At first, I was very grateful for the provision of their catering. After being stuffed with a lot of different items that I rarely overate, I became nauseous.

After having food forcefully stored in the cells and organs of my body, I was allowed to sit for a digesting process. I was starting to feel so much better about everything, beginning with my body. The food settled in. The pain was not as stressful as before. The tease of pleasure left me with the strength of endurance. Even better, I was led back into the shower for another cleansing. Even with being set free from tied hands, I still had no use for them. The women surrounding me did it all. Soaking and rinsing every inch of my body. If I was once lacking the feeling of being a King before, that most definitely wasn't an issue now. I definitely had a kingly sense of mind. I even felt relief from the bore of bondage, as I am right now. I don't think I could be any freer.

Once the showers were over, the many Queens escorted me into the wardrobe and dried me off. Rubbed me down in oils that were potent with redolence. They dressed me in comfortable clothing. A thin Nike sweatsuit and running shoes. My hair, which had grown a medium length from all the months that went by without a haircut, was braided to the back in a number of seven braids.

Afterwards, the escorts were back to their travels. Four in front of me and four behind me. They walked in perfect pairs like marching soldiers. I was stuck in the middle like Malcolm, forced to keep moving. Not allowed to slack in a step. It was a ceiling-to-floor bookcase or that's what I had mistaken it to be. A book was pulled halfway out in a diagonal position. The trap door slid open revealing a tortuous staircase. Without procrastination, the leading four women made their way down the stairs. I was compelled to follow as the four women behind me forcibly reminded me of their presence.

The trip seemed like forever. Maybe because it was so quiet and dark. The only light visible was from the circle window on the ceiling. The farther we traveled down the stairs, the darker it got. Finally, we had reached an ending making it to the bottom. Not here again I thought to myself. I had a belief that the sky had no limits. Now, I question the limitlessness of the bottomlessness. Just how far was one willing to let himself fall? Now on top of the quietness that had intensified with eerie, the darkness that had deepened with the denseness, was a cold spooky temperature. You know I had questions but had long ago given up on asking them. But remember when I asked you how far was one willing to let himself fall? A door had opened. I knew because I heard the squeaky sound of the henges, although I couldn't see. "Through this door and down that hallway is your route towards true freedom. See you on the other side, King." I recognized the voice to be Shayemanes. I walked through the door and immediately it was slammed shut. I faced it in an attempt to open it. There wasn't even a doorknob to be found in the depressing darkness. I even kicked and banged on the door, but it was all for no reason at all. I faced back towards the direction I was directed to take, dropped my nuts, and faced my fears. The hallway was extremely narrow and a distance of about twenty yards, and then … "Wat da!?... Oh shit …" The hallway ended in a steep slope like one of those steel sliding boards. Guess I was about to get a taste of the depths of that bottom.

Chapter 32: No Flex Zone
Scene: Jackson Ward

Back to my stomping grounds. I'm standing on ten. Never in my life have I ever run from shit except 12. There wasn't a need to start now. As a matter of fact, nowadays, I won't be running from the pigs either. Y'all knew that though. I had the old lady drop me off at the dealership. I copped a brand-new Dodge Challenger. The Drag Pak joint 426. Paid in full. Covered in red paint; of course, with slime green accessories. Right now, the gear was in park as I sat behind the wheel. St. Paul was the street. The same exact spot where I spilled my brother's blood out into the field of our home turf. For the first time, I was in deep thought about the situation. I found myself pondering on questions such as did I really have to play my hand the way I did? Or did I have options? Truthfully, the answers were no and yes. On the other hand, now was not the time for regrets or sympathy. It was too late. I felt that in order for me to make my books, I had to set Q's bid back. Shit was cutthroat.

As I looked over to my left, I realized just how much my thoughts had me lacking off course. A police car, which we called a 'black and white,' had pulled up right alongside my whip. My windows were rolled up. They were also slightly tinted. Enough not to notice that it was me in the car. All the windows on the black and white were rolled up as well. The passenger window dropped about a third of the length. I reached for my gun with my left hand from the side door and placed it in my lap. My intention was redirected when I noticed the higher-up ponytail and freshly arched eyebrows of the passenger. It was Lil Shawty. Some other police bitch who I've never seen before was the driver. I dropped my window at about the same distance as Lil Shawty. She gave me a sly look that said fuck me. She then tossed a cellular flip phone through my window and blew me a kiss. Next, the wheels of the car were carrying her away.

The first thing I did was rolled my window up while look-ing around to see if anyone saw what just happened. Surprisingly and luckily for them, there was no one around because I may have had to shoot their eyes out. After taking a few seconds off the clock of life, I noticed someone coming out of a hallway on the brickyard front where Q used to hustle. Even at a distance, I caught the drip of her walk. I knew exactly who it was. I looked at the phone in my hand and realized there was a note attached. I detached the note and read it. There was an address and time of meeting. I flipped the phone open and searched the contacts. There was only one number logged under a nameless save. I banged the phone closed, slid it into my pocket, tucked my pistol, and hopped out of the car.

"Damn Boo, you looking' like you tryin' to snatch a nigga off da market." I approached from the rear end of my car.

"Do all you niggas use da same game?" she asked.

"Oh, naw baby. I'm da one and only. Ain't no nigga like me."

"Yeah, I know. Dey all say dat shit too."

At first, we were both heading towards each other. Upon her last comment, she walked straight past me. As she did, I took a couple of steps backwards before spinning on my heel to walk beside her. "Fuck all dat. I'm tryin' to figure out where you goin' all sexy and dolled up?" I spit a little more game hoping to poison her with my venom. Usually, by now I would have a bitch in the bag at the sight of my approach. But this one was playing hardball and I think I knew why.

"I'm goin' to mind my business and stay da fuck out of yours."

"Shidd, Ion mind you in mine. Matter of fact, I'm tryin' to give you da business."

She sucked her teeth. "Boy, please. All you give me is a headache."

"Wat, you need a cushion on yo headboard?" I got you." She paused at her car. For the first time, she set her sights on me. At first, it was a look of disgust. Then it turned sadden-like. Regardless of the emotion, I knew then that I had her by some type of attachment. She shook her head before traveling around the front end of her. She climbed into the golden Saturn and trapped herself inside without a word, without a gesture, she was pulling away from the curb.

Shawty was a little thicker than what I remembered. She was still sexy as hell though. Come to think about it, I think the weight added some sex appeal to her physique. I wonder if it was that hard for Q to bag the bitch. At the thought of him fucking her, a wave of jealousy and envy washed over me, drowning me in the thirst of lust. I'll get her in due time.

Chapter 33: Reggie Bad Azz
Scene: The Hallway

What the fuck do you keep following me for? Are you trying to get slumped or some? Nigga ain't trying to do no talking. Shit, just all fucked up. I shouldn't have even come back around this bitch. I had just come from across the water over the South, seeing my kids. Maine, look, if you gone stand right here, you gone have to get in the cut. I'm on the run and ain't trying to make the hallway hot. Come in closer. Duck off with AG.

See, I told you 12 coming down the Paul right now. I'm glad you listened to a nigga 'cause I ain't taking no prisoners or leaving witnesses. Hold on, they are stopping. Even though the hallway was starting to block my sight, I could hear the squeaks of the brakes. I peeped around the corner of the hallway and used it as a shield. For the first time, I noticed that a blood-red Dodge Challenger dripping in slime green venom was parked at the curb. I wondered who was in the car just because of the kit of the body alone. Whoever it was had to be unique and paid. I also wondered how long the car had been there. That's the thing about these project cuts and hallways. You never knew who would be right around the corner, which was exactly why I loved to use them in my favor.

I stood staring at the car dripping in drips of snake venom. It flooded a quarter of the bottom part of the car. In between drips were different versions of snakes. I fucked with how the Black Mamba slid directly down the middle of the hood. I was trying to see what 12 was doing. They had parked directly beside the slimed-out ride. I could see the passenger of the police car. That was it. She was a bad bitch with a skin tone like caramel. I caught how Shawty looked at whoever was in the driver's seat of the slime. It was flirtatious. Something flew out the window of the black and white and landed in the other car. Shawty blew a kiss then the car pulled off.

Now my antennas were way up. I knew whoever this cheese-getting ass nigga was, wasn't a rat. He was definitely fucking whoever was in that police car. I made my way to the third floor. I guess you already know because I see you still following me. To keep it one hundred, you're kind of cool though. I'm fucking with you. As I was on my way into an apartment, someone from across the hallway across the building was coming out of an apartment on the third floor. She was bad too. I wondered how I never saw her out here before. I knew damn near everybody out here. I watched her come down the steps until she started to make her way down the sidewalk. I thought about hollering at her, but I was on the hunt right now.

Chapter 34: Dawn's Distinctiveness
Scene: Brickyard Front

It was already a rare occasion that I saw the sun. Most times I only caught the peak of it. Whenever the opportunity presented itself, I would invest pleasure minutes gazing into the sun while calming the thoughts of my mind. With all the clutters on my mind, one thing I definitely needed was to decalcify it. Right now, life as I knew it was calling me to duty. I had decided to take a giant leap of faith today. Stepping out of the shadows of the moon. I was on my way to Virginia Commonwealth University in hopes of setting up payments to get me back into school.

Ladies, you know that feeling when your sixth sense is tingling? That deep intuition that alerts you of a man with dry intentions. On the approach with a thirst for the juices in your box? Right, which was one reason I hated coming outside. Why did being so beautiful have to be such a curse? I knew I was a bad bitch. I didn't need niggas drooling all over me with their tongues hanging out to confirm it. Especially not this one.

If you lived out here and didn't know who Flex was, then you were living under a rock. Hell, even I knew of the nigga while living under a rock. It wasn't long after meeting Q, and Flex coming home, that I had put the pieces together of their relations. The first time I saw them together was the first time I was caught off guard by Q's surprise visit to the strip clubs I danced in. From that night on, I watched Flex closely every chance I got. Just trying to figure him out. Unexpectedly, that wasn't hard to do. I concluded that he was a selfish, slimy snake and I didn't trust him as far as I could bury him. At times, my sixth sense even advised me to put Q up on certain things that I'd noticed about his so-called beloved brother. Q being the more complicated to understand, kind of made me nervous as to what his reaction may be. You know how some of these niggas be. 'Bro's before hoes.' Using slogans and codes that didn't match their actions.

"Damn, Boo, you lookin' like you tryna snatch a nigga off da market." He walked around the back of his car. I can't say which was slimmer about the nigga, his motives or the car. Maybe they both reflected a perfect illustrative unity between the two.

Anyway, cutting all the small talk, I dubbed the nigga without giving it a second thought. Flex disgusted me. After talking with him for the first time, I now understand why. I don't know if he knew that I was fucking Q before he passed away. I'm pretty sure he did. If so, he definitely didn't give a fuck. I'm almost certain that he didn't know that I had a member of his bloodline developing inside my womb. Most likely he didn't. I was almost sick of hearing his childish game and was just about to smack the shit out of him to shut him up. However, when I looked up at him to get an aim at my target, I noticed how much he resembled Q. His skin tone was lighter, eyes were brighter, but damn... He was actually a sex nigga. It saddened me to see that go to waste. Twice. Once here with Flex and his ugly ways and second with the passing of Q. Even though he was gone, I would remain loyal to him as if he still remained. Now that's a true bad bitch.

I left that nigga Flex to stand there and flirt with himself. I got into my car and couldn't wait to pull off. As I did, I noticed someone creeping from the back of one of the buildings. With a big pistol in his tote. I hoped that whoever the person was preying on Flex. If so, I prayed he got whatever he deserved. As for me, I thanked God for allowing me to make an exit in pursuit of my destination.

Chapter 35: Reggie's 33
Scene: St. Paul Street

I entered the front door of the apartment and exited out the back. That way I could creep closer to the car from the cut. My hand was already gripping the Glock .23 that carried 33 shots. I called this bitch my bull. It always came through in the clutch and together we were like Jordan and Pippen. I let a car roll past before I decided to pop out from around the corner. When the car made it at least half a distance to the corner, I upped the bull and quickly stepped into stealth mode.

My intended target was to run upon the car. That was until I noticed that a nigga was leaning on the trunk of it. Remaining unnoticed, I slid up on the dude and pressed the pistol to the back of his head. "Nigga, if you move I swear to God, it's gone be the last move you gone make." I walked around to face my target to find out it was Flex.

"Reggie," Flex sucked his teeth. "You know a nigga ain't never get dat close up on me with a tool before right?" He was nonchalant like I wasn't a certified stepper out of this bitch. "Get dat shit out my face fool."

"Oh, damn Flex, I ain't know dat was you my nigga!" I tucked the .23 under my Louie V belt. "Was dat you 12 was fuckin' wit like dat?" I asked even though I already knew now.

"Yeah. Dat was da lil bitch I told ya'll niggas I was fuckin'."

"Oh, dat's Lil Shawty? Yeah, dat bitch bad."

Flex paused and looked up at me. "Have you seen her?"

"Yeah. She just rolled down Da John." I lied. "Wat's up though? Where have you been? You think it's safe to sit out here like dis? You know niggas ain't been feeling you lately out here?"

"Yeah, I know' brah. Ion give a fuck. Dis my hood too, fool. If niggas feel some type of way, dey either slay da beast or get sprayed."

I've always known Flex to have an I don't give a fuck attitude. But that was on some of them vs us shit. Now, it seemed as if it was us vs us when it came to him. His recent actions have been plucking my nerves for a while now. I gave the game to the little nigga. Now he was trying to play me with it. The only thing that beat a cross was a double cross. I couldn't tell yet if he would actually cross me. I wasn't gone give him a chance to show me either.

For real, for real, the little nigga was so deadly that I thought about dropping his ass right here. Right now. Give his ass the whole .33. I did see some fucked-up shit out here. I don't want to sound fucked up in the head, but I swear I had a small hunch that this nigga killed Q. Even if it was a small hunch. If he would smoke his own brother, I probably didn't have to ask if he would cross me.

A phone started ringing. You could tell from the ringtone that it wasn't a Smartphone. Flex pulled the flip out and opened it. That must have been what I saw coming out of that window. Quickly, Flex flipped the phone back closed, slid it into his pocket, and headed for the car. "I gotta slide right quick. Be back fool." He said opening the car door.

"Shidd, wat's up? Let me slide with you." I was trying to rock the cradle. Hold the baby close.

"Naw, I'm good. Dis shit is personal," he said before hopping in the car and pulling off. He was smart. But I was on his head now. The only way to catch a snake was to play one.

Chapter 36: No Flex Zone Part II
Scene: St. Paul Street

Sitting on the trunk of my car, I contemplated a concrete plan to regain some type of control over the camp. All this thinking shit had me maladjusted. I was just used to doing shit. What was there to think about? As soon as I thought about getting up, I felt the cold steel of someone's pistol on the back of my head. See what I mean about over-thinking? This was the second time in a few minutes that I got caught lacking due to brainstorming. Guess it was a time and place for everything. Whoever the predator was, spoke some cold words with ease. I knew that he was definitely a killer. All I knew was that he had better make sure he finished the job.

I found out that it was Reggie who had the gun to my head. Once he realized that he had made an honest mistake, he tucked his pistol. That was his second mistake. What does this nigga think, I'm a victim or something? Did he not know that I was fucked up in the head and was a long way from trusting a soul? Yeah, that nigga thinks you're soft. Nigga, you are soft. If that was me, I would have clipped that nigga as soon as he dropped that gun. On top of dealing with this shit from Reggie, I had this voice in the back of my head encouraging me to do what I already wanted to do anyway. I wanted to tell that voice to shut the fuck up. But I couldn't get caught in another one of my psychotic states in public. That would make me look weak as a leader. Instead, I faked a conversation with Reggie. He mentioned some shit about niggas not feeling me. You know that shit pissed me off. To my own surprise though, I maintained my composure.

Saved by the bell, well ring, I knew it would be dumb to answer the phone in front of bad azz. I wasn't sure which side of the field he was playing on just yet. Soon, I would test his loyalty. I made some lame excuse to excuse myself and he went for it. I missed the first call but as soon as I got back in the car, a second ring was buzzing. I accepted the call, put the phone to my ear, but said nothing. From the other end of the phone, she giggled. It was Lil' Shawty. "Don't get scared now punk," she joked.

"I ain't scared of shit but happiness," I told her as I whipped the steering wheel pulling away from the curb.

"Wat?" she asked with confusion expressed in her tone.

"Anyway. What's good? I see you makin' major moves out here in des streets." I was referring to the phone.

"Yeah. Thanks, fo da motivation." She replied. "It's a secured line. Untraceable except by me of course, and it's almost impossible to tap. One thing I cannot have you doing though is making me call back-to-back. When this phone rings, you need to know it's me and it's important.

"My bad Lil' Shawty. I got you though. Nigga was jus in da middle of taking care of some at da time."

"Some more important than me?"

"Ion know, it's hard to tell right now. One thing I can say is that you are quickly climbing up my scale of impatience."

She laughed goofily in my ear. "I hate you."

"That's good. I like that."

"Wat? Why would you want me to hate you?"

"Cuz at least that way, I can't break yo heart."

"Hmm." Was followed by a short pause. "Whatever. Anyway, you better not break the schedule. Time. Place. Be der, or I'ma break yo dick off. Oh, and bring money fo payments. It costs to be da boss Daddy." She ended the call with a flirtatious laugh. I was already on my way.

Chapter 37: Q Back In The Grave
Scene: The Abyss

The slope was long but hastened in speed caused by the pull of gravity. When it ended, my body slammed to the underground surface. I found myself boxed in a cubical shape room that was walled with mirrors. I'm talking about every inch. Every corner, including the ceiling along with the very ground I stood on. On the surface of things, there seemed to be no way out. The only logical solution for me was the way I dropped in. However, trying to climb back up the narrow slippery slope was damn near impossible. As much as I hated to use that word, the attempts were energy-draining and caused fatigue. I gave up on that plan. If that was my route out, I'd probably die down here staring at the reflection of self. What I saw was a book bag. In that bag were tools. A rope, one empty canteen, and … books. Two of them, well, three of them were familiar. They were The Torah, The Bible, and the Quran. The last tool in the bag was an actual one. It was a hammer.

I considered the book bag and the tools in it to be useless at a time like this. What the fuck was I supposed to do, read myself to death? I was starting to think that the idea was to save my soul through the choice of one or maybe all of the religious books. That's when it hit me, I did something that I haven't done in a long time now. Said a prayer. With my head pressed to the mirrored floor, I practically begged for the help of God. Who else could I depend on to get me out of this indescribable antidote? "Allah, please provide me with strength, guidance, endurance, tools, knowledge, wisdom, and power to make it out of dis. Please forgive me for every sin I've ever committed through action, utterance or thought. And if these are my final moments on this earth inside this body, that you have greatly blessed me with, then I want to thank you with all that I have fo bringin' me this far."

Before disconnecting my head from the floor, I opened my eyes and was once again face to face with me. Getting up, I tried my best to gather my thoughts. What was I to do next, sit and wait on a sign? A miracle? Of the Angel Gabriel to show up? What would Jesus do? What would anybody do in this predicament? What would you do? I ain't ask for this. At least I thought I didn't. Time as I knew it was no longer thought of in the same sense as before. As seconds ticked away from a soundless watch, the equilibrium of my mind was way off balance. So much so, that the thought of going crazy, drove me crazy. Thoughts of insanity wouldn't free me either though. Even if I wasn't confident.

I loved me some me. But I was getting sick of only seeing me. On top of that, there were so many of me. Lonely me, helpless me, useless me, and stupid me. Those weren't the mess I fell in love with though. So, did I really love me or the masquerade of me? With that thought appeared the angry me. I shuffled through the book bag again in an attempted search. I was left standing, holding a hammer in my hand. Hold up. A hammer? I was surrounded by mirrors. There was nothing more I'd rather do right now than shattering the image of myself. I took a couple of steps back and threw the hammer as hard as I could at the opposition. The mirror across from me collapsed like one of the Twin Towers. In effect, the ceiling mirror was coming down at an angle making its way to the floor. The other three mirrored walls lost the support of each other. I pushed into the one I was closer to, sending it to the ground. Thankfully, only a few steps forward and I was clear of the crashing ceiling. Although pieces of glass ricocheted off the floor everywhere along with the tumbling walls.

I took a look around with an awe-stricken countenance. Flaming torches settled along the circular wall in perfect order and placement. I counted twelve. A chandelier in the shape of a five-point hung burning above my head. I was in a cave. Ain't that some shit? I have gone from a cell to a cave. It was very spacious and large. Dry and warm. Yet, I had no urge for water. I noticed a section with Persians rugs and fluffy pillows. Burning candles surrounded the area. Leaning up against the wall on the opposite side of the cave was a broom. How amazing I thought. Still, I tipped-toed my way around the pieces of glass in pursuit of the broom.

After sweeping up the glass into a big pile, I shook off all the remaining glass from the book bag. I grew terrified when I heard an echoed slam. "Wat da fuck was dat?" I asked myself of course. From the very same slide, I dropped in to shout out a cylinder tube. I looked around in search of a camera or something that may have been watching me. "How da fuck?" I picked up the tube and pulled out the rolled-up sheet of paper. It read:

Now that you have passed your first test, 'The shattering of your ego,' you must learn and listen

for the language of God. Study the laws of the perfected universe that was crafted by His hands and

the creative word 'Be.' From here, you will be left alone to transverse your journey. The only advice I

am allowed to provide you with, is that, all that's lost is found within self.

Even though physically, I was, I no longer felt alone. I grew in confidence that someone somewhere was watching over me. With the bag in tote, I made my way over to the matted area. Taking a seat, I found it to be very comfortable and relaxing. I laid the books out in front of me, along with the empty canteen. Lost in the moment, I looked around for a sign, a clue. What I noticed were folded pieces of paper in each of the glass candle bases. There were only two problems. One was that the paper was actually trapped inside the glass. Second, was that in order to break into the glass, I would have to extinguish the fire of the candle. Without a second thought, I blew out one of the candles. Displacing the hammer back out of the bag, I laid the candle base on the ground and gave it a tap. The glass shattered and I was able to retain the paper.

Ephesians 6:10-13 was all the paper read. At least I was now getting somewhere. Flipping through the pages of the New Testament, I searched for the listed book. Once found, I read it. "10. Finally, be strong in the Lord and in His mighty power. 11. Put on the full armor of God, so that you can take your stand against the devil's schemes. 12. For our struggle is not against flesh and blood, but against the rulers, against the authorities, against the powers of this dark world, and against the spiritual forces of evil in the Heavenly realms."

Oh ok. That was deep, but it still ain't get me out of here. I killed another flame and cracked another candle base. This one is from the Quran Al-Kauthar (Abundance/A River in Paradise) 108. It read, "verily we have granted you Al-Kauthar (A river in paradise). Therefore, turn in prayer to your Lord and sacrifice to Him only. For he who hates you will be cut off (from posterity and every good thing in this world in the hereafter.)"

The next one was from the Old Testament in the Book of Isaiah 52: 14-15. "14. Just as there were many who were appalled at Him, His appearance was so disfigured beyond that of any human being and his form marred beyond human likeness. 15. So he will sprinkle many nations and kings will shut their mouths because of Him. For what they are not told, they will see, and what they have not heard, they will understand."

This went on for some time until all the fires of the candles were vapored into their smoking forms. More glass to clean up and more holy words shifting between the three books. I had an understanding like never before. The last scripture came from Revelation 12:7. "Then war broke out in Heaven. Michael and his Angels fought against the dragon and the dragon, and his angels fought back."

Chapter 38: Flex the Establishment
Scene: The Meeting Place

I still held all the keys to the main doors in the hood. Wether niggas liked it or not, I was still the landlord out of this bitch. They would have to respect that fact or get laid flat. I would not hesitate to pop any opp who attempted to oppose my will. Everything was mine for the taken. I was more than willing to go and get it.

The time had come for me to arrive at the meeting spot. As I spoke, I was pulling up right now. You know I'm on some super top-secret shit, so I refuse to let you know the exact location. All I can say was that it was a warehouse. The wildly impractical part is that it wasn't even abandoned. Damn near fully occupied. At first, I thought, set up until I realized that by now I had Lil Shawty in too deep. Besides, if this bitch was planning to set me up, before I die, I'll make sure to put a bullet in that bitch's head.

I pulled around the back of the warehouse where there was almost little to no traffic at all. Lil Shawty stood alone outside of an open garage door. She spotted me, waved me over, and disappeared into the garage. I drove my car into the space almost as soon as the door was sliding closed from top to bottom. It's all or nothing now I guess. Light gave the darkness of the garage a place to hide. In addition to that, it provided a vision for my eyes to see that the garage was set up like some type of office. It had cubicles, computers, an office desk, a dry board, maps of the city, pictures of police officers and all types of other shit.

"Hey Daddy." Lil Shawty greeted, always flirting. "You like?"

"Yeah. I'm feeling da determination. But wats all dis shit fo? And who da fuck is he?" He was a short darky looking nigga with glasses. He sat behind one of the desks which looked to me like the main one.

"He is part of the team. Our computer tech and operator. He is in control of tracking all patrol cars. Catching codes and dispatch and alerting us of all crimes that are reported throughout da city."

"Throughout da city?"

"Yeah crazy. Wat you think, we gone go dis hard and not go all da way. Come here." She ordered me over to the side of whoever the fuck he was. "One," she said to … He. "Show me."

"One?" I questioned in puzzlement.

"Yeah. He's one and she's two." Lil Shawty pointed to the policewoman who I recognized as the driver from earlier. I had already seen how sexy her face was. She had this pretty ratchet look. The popping bubble gum type, which she was doing now. Seeing the body that matched the beauty had my mind all off the business at hand. I ain't care that she was 12. If I could fuck one police bitch, I could fuck two.

"Hey!" Two said with her project barbie tone. Without saying a word, one was pulling up different shit on the computer. He showed me camera spots around the city. The tracking of police cars as they cruised or sat. Places where crimes were taking place at this moment. Police on duty, and times of their shift change. Rocks of background history on police and criminals. He even pulled me up. A gangster.

"He can do all dis and more." Lil Shawty confirmed. "And she will be with me. We are putting plans together to recruit more. But fo now, this will have to do. Besides, we don't want to alert da wrong person and they tip us off. As far as one and two go." I laughed in my head. One and Two. They were 12.

"Their wish is to remain anonymous."

"I just want to get paid fo real. Dis money ain't cutting it." Two interrupted.

"Ight look." I finally took the floor. I had to establish that I was the captain of this boat. That it would sail by my order. "Now dat I know who and what we got; Ima put some missions in to play fo y'all to complete. I must warn you dat shit can get reckless at da strike of a match. For dat reason, I find it substantial dat commands be respected. Demands be met. That the line of betrayal doesn't get crossed. Make no mistakes about it, you are on da other side of da field now. Once you cross dat line, ain't no turning around. With me you can take yo destiny to da top. Become Lieutenants or whatever yo wishes maybe. Riches or whatever, or

I can send you to da grave wit regrets, dat you didn't take advantage of dis opportunity."

"Boy!" Lil Shawty cut me off. We'll really not really because I was done anyway. "You don't even have to do all dat. I got dem and we got you."

"Good. I'm glad you know dat. So, if one of dem crosses us, you takin da fall." All Lil Shawty did to my response was sucked her teeth. She had an alarmed look on her face as if she was realizing for the first time that she had just made a deal with the devil himself. I walked the short distance to my whip and came back with three envelopes in hand. I had more just in case. I gave each one of them to my new employees. "Dis is da investment. Da better da work, da better da interest."

"Dis wat I'm talking about," Two said.

"Ok, so wat do you want us to do til you come up with des plans of yours?" Lil Shawty wanted to know.

"First off, keep 12 from round me. Let me know if I'm headed in der direction or vice versa. I want y'all to pick up all calls coming out of Gilpin Court. Dat way, we can see who is tipping while leaving dem stranded with no help. I also need y'all to dig deep and figure out a way to put a clean-up team together. Da less evidence, da less cases. Can ya'll handle dat?" I was talking to all but looking at Lil Shawty.

"Got you daddy. Piece of cake."

Chapter 39: Q's Outbreak

I read through all the scriptures noted. Even doubled back on a few of them. I couldn't find a single sign or clue as to how to get the fuck out of this cave. They all sound as if they are preparing me for something. But nothing told me something of what I needed to hear now. At one point, I found myself bored and read through random contents of the books. Eventually, I was being driven back to my old state of anxiety. I started to move around the cave. I banged on shit with the hammer, trying to feel for secret switches. Even pulled on the torches on the wall. I found nothin. I was like a non-existent second away from going insane. I was now at the point where I was bouncing off the walls of the cave, trying to climb up them heading to the top of nowhere. Losing fatigue again. I found myself with my knees buried into the floor of the cave with an agoraphobic spirit. I looked up to the ceiling searching for the face of God.

"How much longer do I have to suffer?" I screamed out as loud as I could hearing only the echo of my voice in response. "Please..Help..Me.." As I looked up at the Pentagram Star glowing in burning flames, in the middle of the rope that attaches the star from the ceiling dangled a shining key. I rose from my knees in contemplation on a way to get the key. Instantly, I remembered that I had a rope. I grabbed the rope and unraveled it. At one end of the rope, was a ready-made noose. I paused for a quick second to process a thought. If they thought for one minute that I would go out in suicide, that was a minute wasted. Back to the task at hand. I swung the noose end of the rope in a circle above my head resembling a cowboy on the hunt for a bull. As strong as I could, I threw it up towards the burning chandelier. The rope flew up in the air and wrapped around the rope that hung from the ceiling. I got a good grip on the rope that I held. With all my might, I pulled at the chandelier. To my surprise, the chandelier came down towards me with extreme ease. As it did, a secret door to the cave revealed itself by sliding upwards as the Pentagram Star came down. I pulled on the rope like a game of tug of war and was soon able to get my hands on the key.

I was so happy to have the key in hand and see a way out of the cave, that I released the rope from my grasp. Just as easy as it came down, the Pentagram Star chandelier went back up twice as fast. As the star went back up to its resting place, the door of the cave slammed back to the ground. This time I grabbed the rope, tied it tight to one of the torches, gathered the tools I was provided, and got the fuck out of that cave.

Through the door of the cave was like a tunnel. Underground of course. I traveled through the tunnel and was met with a dead end. After seeing all that I've seen though, I didn't expect that to be true. I pushed on what acted as a wall and found that it was a large stone. Now out of the tunnel, that same stone blocked my path to continue my journey. I pushed the stone back into its original place and was free to proceed. However, what I saw made me want to second-guess my next movement.

For one, it was hot as hell. I meant literally hot as hell. For two, I don't know how the hell it was possible, but fire burned everywhere around me. Skulls and bones were left over from what I guess to be the ones who couldn't travel through the pits of hell. Ironically, there actually was a way out. Unfortunately, the only way out of the fire was through it. At least, there were options. There were two. One was a brimstone path laid out over to the far end. The second was a bridge of flames on each side of the railings right ahead of me. I was tempted to take the latter. But the bridge seemed weak dangling over on an even deeper pit of fire. It was also narrow and left, with almost no room to protect your skin from the flames. It was so hot that as I stood my distance, it felt as if my shoes were melting on my feet. I was forced to take them off before the material burned my feet.

Other than suffering from dehydration, I figured that I had little time to plan out my decision. I was wrong though. The sound of a hissing snake crept from the rear of me. I turned around frightfully just to make sure that I wasn't tripping. Nope. I wasn't tripping. It was definitely a snake. It wasn't an anaconda, but you couldn't convince me of that. Whatever it was, that bitch was big. Without even knowing, I dropped everything that wasn't attached to me as I ran for my life. I didn't even bother to look back, but I could tell from the slithers of the snakes sliding, that it was moving fast. I made my way to the hot brimstones and high-stepped my way across the other side. I hadn't realized it until I was on common ground, but my fucking feet were on fire. I'm not even sure how I had the strength to stand on them. On the other side of the fire, the snake was smart enough not to follow my path.

I searched for a way out and found the next path with ease. It was a long dry distance. I was so thirsty and desperate for water that I could smell it in the air that my nose hadn't deceived me, I came upon a thin stream of water. For a moment, I almost regretted leaving the empty canteen behind. However, I refused to let that stop me. I double-cuffed the palms of my hands and dipped them into the flowing fluid. "Umm." It was so refreshing. I don't know if it was because I was so thirsty, had just left a dry cave, and went through the blazing fire that made the water seem so... Pure. I now had a newfound respect for water. Matter of fact, the taste was familiar. It wasn't the taste of water; it was the very same taste of the river in my dream where my Pops had come to visit me. The liquid, whatever it was, seemed as if it gave me a new life. I know what you are probably saying right? How many lives does this nigga have? I won't act as if I have all the answers when the shit is new to me as well. All I knew is that at this very moment, my heart rate was decelerating. I felt sparkles of electricity tingling in my brain. Could free energy literally vibrate throughout my body as I deeply breathe in the air that provides natural nutrients to my organs? I felt like a machine built by God.

I continued to travel down the path of the underground river. Only stopping to fill my liver with more of the miracle water. On my gallivant, I noticed how the stream became wider the further along I went. It turned into a full body of water almost like a small sea. With no bridge or boat, the only way through it was to dive in. Thank God I know how to swim. Whoever said Black people couldn't should exclude me. My brother and I had been diving in the deep end since as far back as I could remember. I was unsure as to how deep this sea of water was, but I didn't waste time procrastinating. I only stuck my feet in first. Before I knew it, the water was up to my neck. I took off with slow and steady strokes, swiftly propelling my body across the body of water. As I came over with my right arm in preparation to make another push, it smacked into something floating in the water. I was forced to stop my motion. I rested my body at ease allowing it to float as well. I went to lift whatever it was out of the water. The object was heavy like dead weight. That's exactly what it was. A dead body. I released the corpse from my hands and pushed it as far out of my way as possible. If I didn't want to end up a decoration for this earth-size fish tank, I had to keep moving.

Chapter 40: Flex Me vs Me
Scene: On my Way

I was on my way back from the projects, again, this time, I ain't care for a plan. I was just going to go with the flow and turn it into cash. I needed more, and fast. I had a nice amount of work in the bag in the back. Now that I basically had control of the flow of law patrol, I could flat the work myself and sell it. I ain't need an army. I was my only competition. Literally.

As I slid through the city, I was bumping that Bagg 'Me vs Me.' That's how I felt right now. No matter how many enemies I eliminated or how isolated I tried to remain, it was hard to escape me. Back in the hotel, I told myself that I would have to live with me. I was more than willing to do that now. It just didn't make any sense to go against myself. Who I truly was. Besides, together, I think we made a nice invincible duo.

Alright, so this is what the move is. First, I was going to re-establish The Carter Ward. I think I wanted to change its name. Instead of no flex zone, how about we call it, exactly that? The Flex Zone. Since I was the muscle and that's where I would push most of my weight anyway. Can't forget the fact that I'm ready to super flex on these niggas with this paper I'm about to make. So, yeah, I liked that. The Flex Zone. Anyway, back to the rundown. I'm going to hit The Kitchen, break down some work, and stretch it as far as I can. Fuck it. Nigga ain't seeing me out that bitch. I'm pretty sure they were still pressing for cash and low on work. Like I said, I was in my own competition.

Next, of course, I was going to post up. There was no time to waste. I'd have to worry about finding a plug and all that other shit later. For now, I had to focus on my surroundings. I pulled up to Bakers Street one way. Money Bagg Yo had one more thing to say through the big speakers before the car cut off. 'I ain't never ran from a nigga (ever). If I did cut my legs off (right now)." I hopped out of my slime and headed towards my destination.

Chapter 41: Q Out the Mud
Scene: The Bottom

For a second, I thought this pool of refreshments would never end. Thankfully, I had another reason to be grateful. I pulled myself out of the water. The ground I landed on was muddy and smelly. Truthfully, it smelled like shit. The spots that I stepped through were knee-deep. As I looked around though, there were heaps of piles everywhere. Some were even taller than me. Standing tall like mountains. Unlike the other life-threatening obstacles that I had to triumph over, this land of mud had no sense of direction, for I don't know how long. I wiggled and wiggled my way through the mud. Desperately, I searched for something that could give me at least a hint. All I found though were more dead bodies. How am I not surprised by that? One could die just from the foul odor alone. There should have been a gas mask in that book bag.

Never becoming stagnant in my movements, I spotted something that I hadn't seen in a very long time. A small circular beam, almost a dot of natural sunlight. I know it may seem unreal, but you should really, really believe me. Like really. Again, I find it important to remind you that I absolutely had no idea how all of this was taking place. Maybe my physical eyes were telling tales. If that was the case, then my words were true to what my eyes thought they saw.

The spec of light came from up high which I assumed to be the surface of the Earth's ground. I found myself again staring into the light searching for salvation. The only way towards the light of direction was to go up. The only way I would be able to do that was to climb the highest mountain of mud.

I'd been to war with the police for the respect, freedom, and justice of my people. Betrayed and shot in the head by the one person I was loyal to the most and left for dead. I had been locked away, incarcerated for I don't know how long. Then kidnapped by the same people who held me captive. I was forced into a society without an option to choose from. Made a sex slave and tricked into a cave. I made it through the fires of hell and depths of waters that threatened to drown me like some before me. After all that, I'll be truly damned if I allow this bullshit to cease me from the freedom I've always longed for. By now, I had become a master of overcoming the bottom, and when, not if I made it out of this, I would lose my fear of flying. For now, I know that falling is not all that hard. And getting back up isn't impossible.

Barefoot, soaking wet, with mud sticking to my skin and clothes, I dug in. On my way up the muddy mountains, I used the remains of dead bodies to elevate my climb. I also used the dead bodies as motivation to push my ambition. I refused to be left in a pile; forced to share a grave with those who didn't have the strength, courage, and intellect to make it out. Once I finally made it to the top, after a strenuous ascendance, I concluded that I was only about six feet away from this underground world of torture. Being closer to this hole, I was able to eyeball the measurement of the circumference to be almost half a foot wide. Instead of digging down, I had to dig up, which was hard to do. As I dug, I tried to climb out of the hole while knocking dirt out of my way. As I went up, the dirt came down. Multiple times, I almost fell out of the hole. Once I was able to use all four of my limbs in a union, it made it a little easier. Not too much though. Thankfully, all I needed was a little ease.

I poked my head out of the hold in the ground and deeply gasped for the fresh flowing air. It gave more strength to my body. Just like the water, I now had a newfound respect for the air I breathed. I used my hands to remove the dirt from around my neck making room from my shoulders to push through. I climbed out of the grave and collapsed to the ground from exhaustion.

Chapter 42: Flex Back 2 Flexing
Scene: Jackson Ward/W. Charity Street

I bagged up a bunch of dimes that were barely a point on the scale. My dubs were barely two. I also had a few half and whole grams ready to be sold. The weight was right, but the prices were high for the high. I posted up on one of the streets that surrounded the One Way. West Charity was the opposite street of the One Way. Whenever 911 was dialed, most of the police cars would enter the projects using this street. But now that I had all that shit in my pocket, I could post up anywhere I wanted to. This was literally my hood now. All I had to worry about now was these bitch ass niggas.

Across the street were Hawk, Blu, Red and a couple of other niggas from TNH niggas walking up the block. Hawk starred with a hateful mug but wisely kept it moving. His peons continued to follow. Blu looked and shook his head. Red looked and put his head down. It was a sense of disappointment. I don't know why. It wasn't my fault that all this shit was happening. I mean maybe it was, but I was just playing the cards I was dealt. As long as them niggas didn't come out of their mouths wrong or upped their pistols, I ain't give a fuck what they did. Right now, I was only out here for one reason. That was money. I ain't take my eyes off them niggas until they rounded the corner. Before they did, I dug in my pockets and flashed a handful of blues in their face for motivation. Even when they were gone, I knew that they could spin back around the bin on their feet. Really, they probably were hoping that I ain't get at them first.

I walked down the block and headed towards the other end of the building that TNH just rounded. Looking down Saint Peter Street, I spotted Pam. She was always out here. I don't know if you know her, but she is a top three go-to for friends when it comes to getting rid of packs. Just don't put the work in her hands. "Aye Pam! Come here, let me holla at you." She wasn't doing shit anyway. Looking at the ground slowly walking searching for what I had. She lifted her head and hurriedly paraded towards me.

"Q!... I mean, I called you Q. Flex, wats up my nigga? You look like yo brother. I miss him. Wats up? Wat you got for me?" Pam was pulling up her oversized pants and stood face to face with me. For real, I wanted to smack the shit out of her for calling me Q. I had a mission for her though.

I was ready to hit the hallway before I whipped the pack out. Then I remembered. "Here, hit dis." I gave her one of my makeshift dimes.

"Ight, let me go in one of these hallways and get my shit together."

"Naw, you good. Smoke it right here."

"Wat? Hell naw. I ain't tryna to make shit. Wat if da police roll up da block or some? You trippin'."

"Wat da fuck I say Pam?" I scolded.

"Ight boy, damn! You ain't gotta yell and all dat." Pam stuffed the crack pipe with the drug, sparked an extended flame from one of those cheap lighters, and took a bit of a hit inhaling the smoke deeply. Her eyes got big like they were bulging out of her head as she stared at me. After holding it in for longer than I expected her to, Pam slowly exhaled the smoke. "Oh my God!" She gasped for air. "I ain't had no shit like dat since Q was here. A lil too much bake on it, but dat shit still good." I wish she would get off Q's dick already.

"Bring some plays my way and I'ma take care of you." Lie.

"Shidd... say no more brah. Where you gone be at, right here?"

"Yeah, Ima be right here." She was gone and found out as soon as she came back that I won't be giving her ass shit unless she was ready to pay for it. I knew how the game went, so I didn't need a runner. Once word gets out, I'll have all these fiends wrapped around my fingers. Game time.

Chapter 43: Q I'm Back
Scene: Spring Street

I was able to indicate the exact duration of my recent swoon. All I could say was that I was thankful that the sun still shined its radiant light upon me. Checking my surroundings, I recognized exactly where I was. In the middle of a field; on the block of Spring Street. This is the very field where one of the battles of the South took place throughout the 1800s. This very same location held one of Virginia's deadliest state penitentiaries. Its nickname was 'The Wall.' It got its name because somehow tens or maybe even hundreds of dead bodies were hidden within the walls throughout the prison. Don't believe me, check the history. Ask Google. Just don't ask me how. Shit, I was born in the 90s.

I studied my surroundings in search of a reason for the end of my underground journey landing me in this spot. I only had the opportunity to view this scene from either traveling the bridge above it or glimpsing it from a side street from downtown.

Why was I not surprised to find a cellar-like building hidden deep underneath the bridge? It was covered over with grass making it look like a simple small hill. Upon my approach, I took a few steps back into the ground and was faced with double doors. They were locked. That's when I remembered the only thing that made it out of the elements of the ground below with me. I reached into my now dried up muddy dusty pockets and pulled out the key that stood the test of time. Perfectly, the key fits into the lock of the door, and thankfully, they were open. With suspended hesitation, I walked down a few more steps. Was I scared? I can't really say. I didn't even know what fear was anymore. Once I learned that I could use fear by standing in front of it and pushing me forward. I now looked at it as a secret weapon.

The inside of the chamber was nothing like the cave. It was bigger than a project apartment. It was also plush and lavish. The first thing I looked for was a shower, which I found Right away, I used it. I started by allowing the steaming hot water to rain down on my body before shifting the water to a cold temperature. The freezing water shocked my nerves, awakening my senses to a higher level of consciousness. After getting clean, I searched for some clothes to get fresh in. So many designers to choose from. I kept it simple by picking out a peachy-colored Champion sweatsuit and a pair of all-white Forces. My next necessity was food, and yes, it was a place for that here as well. There were two refrigerators; a mini one and a medium-sized one. I opened the door of the mini-fridge first. What I saw caused my desires to overthrow my needs. Gold bottles of Ace of Spades. All types of flavors of Cîroc. Even my favorites, Hennessy, and Gin. Feeling super brand new, I decided to go for something I never had before and grabbed a bottle of that Spade. It made sense why the top of the mini refrigerator was filled with a cup holder full of shot glasses. I turned around with the bottle and glass in hand anticipating clogging my recent memories with the intoxication.

A hundred and eighty degrees later, I got a taste of the fear that I thought I had forgotten about. My heart skipped a beat causing my body to vault. As a reaction to my actions, both the glass and bottle slipped out of my hands crashing to the floor. The glass shattered while the bottle bounced around clinking on the floor. This nigga was sitting at the kitchen table puffing on a Black and Mild as if all shit was noble. I stared at him in confusion, not knowing if I should curse his ass out or hug him.

"I see you pass da trials of yo demons. You're no longer a savage youngin.' In fact, you a couple of steps away from standing over da heights of a man." A proud smirk spread across his face.

"Wat da fuck is all dis shit 'bout Streets'?" I questioned my mentor.

"Long story Q. I'll make it as short as possible, but we gotta get going. Let's move."

"But I ain't get to eat." That didn't matter to Streets obviously as he made his way out of the burial chamber. I made the decision to shut up and follow. Now, I sat shotgun in the passenger seat of the same Range Rover it all started in. As we rode through the downtown section of Richmond City, heading westbound, Streets briefed me on the destiny I never saw coming. It all started with my Pops who had secretly joined the society with hopes that it would make a better life for him, his wife, and first-born son, me. Along the way, the money, power, and rituals drove Pops crazy. Before long, he had reached a certain degree that required a lethal sacrifice. He would have to pay the price with the blood of his own life or his first-born son. He chose for me to stay and carry the legacy, which is why his life was taken despite how the cover-up made it seem. So, to sum it all up in my mind, I was left to clean up the bullshit that he found himself in. The only good part for me was that I wouldn't have to sacrifice. Through the sacrifice of my Pops, my blood was salvaged and as they called it, royal.

Things were starting to make sense now. Everything for that matter. I thought I had power at first, but that was nothing compared to what I know I have, without even knowing I had made it out of the mud of ignorance. Through that very same ignorance, I had become illuminated. My past was dead. The future was unborn. The only life I had to live was right now.

Streets pulled up to a dealership off West Broad Street. Instead of the parking lot, he drove through an oversized doorway that was fit for a car's clearance. Streets hopped out and so did I. "Joe, wats up boss man." Joe returned the compliment before asking, "What's up? You ready for me?"

"Yeah. Wat you got fo me?"

"You said the kid would look good in a Rolls right? Well, check this out!"

"Yeah. Ion want da Lil ma fucka trying to roll around da city matchin' my whip. He already wanna be me so bad." Streets replied while following behind Joe while I followed behind Streets. Joe walked us over to an eggshell, off-white color Rolls Royce. Shit was like that. Fully equipped Presidential tinted windows, shimming24-inch rims. At that moment, all I could do was picture me rolling through the city behind the wheel of that bitch. "Yeah. Dis perfect right here." It was as if Streets' last words were a secret code of some sort. Joe threw me a set of keys with a no-look pass. Being more aware than I've ever been in my life, I caught the key on instinct. "Dis you Q. Pull up let me put you up on some." I followed Streets to the back end of the car. Joe popped the trunk and I saw a clean and empty space. That was until Streets pressed a button that was hidden from plain sight. A slider in the base of the trunk slid open revealing piles of con-cealed bricks. My heart skipped a beat twice in a row before speeding up its rhythm. "I'm already convinced dat you know wat to do wit dis. Just remember, pace and execution." Street reminded me.

"Say no more fool. I got you." I knew no other way to say this except, I'm back!

Chapter 44: Streets Never Forgotten
Scene: In Traffic

What's up with it? If you knew me even just a little bit then you would know I don't talk much. In my world, there wasn't a need to. Plus, when you are a real boss, you let the money talk. Right now, though, I'll spare you a few minutes. Only if you agree to listen. True enough, I stayed focused on my business, but it wouldn't be fair to say I'ma selfish nigga. I'm willing to help anybody that's willing to help themselves first. Don't be mad at me. That's the way God said it should be. That's why I fucked with the little nigga Q. He was never the type out here looking for a handout. But at the same time, not too prideful to take one either. When it hits his hand, whatever Q decides to tell you, that's between y'all. It's things that I refuse to speak on though. All I could say is that I hope he was smart enough to stay away from his brother...

Oh shit! Speaking of Flex, I forgot to warn Q. I switched lanes all the way over to the left jumping into the turning lane. I made a quick U-turn and headed back towards the east driving back into the city. While picking up speed, my phone began to ring. That was rare. When my phone did ring, it was either major money or ... Yeah, it was the second one. "Hello," I answered the call through the speakers of the car.

"Saint James." It was the Grand Master. "Have you provided Jerimiah 13 with his obligations, tasks, and avoidance?" Shit! I was cursing myself out in my head. I will never forget almost anything.

"Yes, Supreme. All except his avoidance. I'm en route as we speak to bring it to his awareness."

"You should hurry Saint James for you know how ambitious our new craftsmen can be. It would be a shame for him to arise from ignorance only to fall into the trap of theoretical suspicion."

"Yes, Supreme. You are right. I will make the correction."

The call was disconnected. I picked up even more speed now, extra anxious to get to Q. I was supposed to tell him two things to avoid before I sent him on his way. One was the Gilpin Court Projects in Jackson Ward. Two were his brother Flex. At least for the time being because they were deadly to his livelihood. How would Q be able to explain popping up after the world considered him dead? How would Flex react to seeing Q after attempting to murder him and failing? Yeah, that's right. We know Flex tried to kill Q. We are, however, unsure if Q knows that for himself. We also know that Flex murdered officers who you may know by their street names Tall and Short. We know that because they were a part of us. They were sent there to rescue Q from his troubles. Flex had bigger plans. His motives weren't drugs or money. It was pure jealousy and hate. Envy because he wanted powers that his older brother had. Don't let this go over your head. Flex is clever and he studied his Pops to a tee. He knows of most of the things he was into. Even when it came to dealing with us. He just couldn't stand on it with proof. He wanted to be a part of it. But he wasn't the chosen one. Q was.

Chapter 45: Q Comes Home
Scene: Jackson Ward

I know symbolically that I had defeated my demons and shattered my ego. But right now, you couldn't tell me shit. I was a ghost in a ghost-getting ghost. For the first time in a long time, I had a reason to laugh. What better way to ease the pain? The only thing was that I knew this moment wouldn't last forever, so, I might as well enjoy it while it was here. I shouldn't even have to tell you where I was pulling up to. Finally, I had the courage to face the music. Matter of fact, I now had the instruments to create the music of my own Lil King.

I turned up the volume to NBA Young Boy's 'Run in Here.' I done died and came back.. And I still see the same thing I done.. died and came back, came back, I see not a damn thing changed. / The words to this song were so much more real to me now. Rolling through the projects, I was gunless, loaded with bricks in the trunk, and without a penny to my name. Almost sounds like old times huh? The difference was that I lacked the fear of death, understood the value of life, and was no longer intimidated by the unjust actions of the law. Besides, I was yet to see a single cop car patrolling the hood as I geared through Gilpin Court. I did notice Flex though, standing there posted all alone as I rode past him. I could see with my mind's eye that life was taking a toll on him. I understood but refused to feel one drop of sympathy. If I haven't learned anything from that brother of mine, it was that when they say, keep your grass cut wasn't enough. This was the jungle. Where we came from, anacondas hung from the trees along with the apes. They glided through the water with the sharks. You need way more than a lawn mower to keep you safe out here. By all means, stay dangerous.

Navigating deeper through the hood, I realized that it was in an even worse predicament than before. Even living in the grave was looking like a better option than its surface. But don't trip by getting too wrapped up in the scene. The real King was back, and in due time, I will take the seat of the throne. Not only will I give the people what they want, but also what they need. First, I had to tie up the loose ends of my bloodline.

Even though I was emotionally detached from my feelings, I just wasn't ready to return to the spot-on Saint Paul Street where Flex tried to turn me into a deceased legend. Therefore, I parked in Saint John. Prior to my return to Jackson Ward, I thought that I would have to duck and hide. Like how would I explain my very existence? Shit was a lot to explain. Even if I found the time to do so, who would be crazy enough to believe me? Being that damn near, the whole project had turned into a ghost town. There was no one to really hide from. I hopped out of the car with the push of a button. Walked up to Keyshia's apartment and knocked on the door.

While waiting on an answer, I heard a voice call out to me. "Excuse me baby." The voice came from over the balcony. I looked down to the first floor and noticed an old-time neighbor. Her name was Ms. Poke. She sat on the porch with her long-time friend, Ms. Buffy. As long as the sun was shining, such as on a day like this one, you could bet that they would be catching the rays. "Hey Ms. Poke. Hey Ms. Buffy. How y'all doing?" I greeted them as normally as possible.

"Oh my…" Ms. Poke started to say before she halfway passed out leaning her body on the frame of Ms. Buffy.

"Child, if you don't get yo tail off me." Ms. Buffy helped Ms. Poke to sit back up properly in her seat. Ms. Poke struggled a little to regain her focus.

"Buffy, do my eyes deceive me, or is dat?"

"Naw, you ain't tripping girl, that's exactly who you think it is. Da boy standin' right in yo face." By this time, I had made my way to the first floor and stood on the porch with the ladies.

"But how on God's green earth? You and I both sat right here da day he got shot in his head." Said Ms. Poke.

"Well Poke, I guess if God is not ready to welcome you home, you have to wait yo turn."

"Q, you look so handsome. If I hadn't known any better, I would have mistaken you for an angel." I smiled. I had to admit, my weight was up. All muscle. The Greeks would say that I had the body of a God. My hair had grown in its length. Although it was snapped up in seven braids. The tone of my skin had a glow. I know I looked different.

"DeQuan, son." Ms. Buffy spoke. "I hate to break da bad news, but if you are looking for Keyshia and yo daughters, you won't find dem round here. Dey been gone fo' some time now."

"Yelp," Ms. Poke chimed in. "Not too long after dat mess happened to you. She was packin' up and headin' out."

"Do you know where to?" I had to ask.

"I think she went ova southside somewhere." Ms. Poke suggested.

"Child, no she didn't. Dat girl off of Old Brook Road somewhere in one of those gated communities." Ms. Buffy added.

"How do you know dat?" Ms. Poke challenged.

"Girl, I just know."

"Well, maybe you're right. All I know is dat she is not around here."

"Well, thank y'all. I appreciate it. Take care of each other." I was stepping off. Couldn't sit long. I already did that enough.

"Dat boy almost lost his life and still ain't learn none. Look at him. I bet he's on his way to his lil side whore house. Shame on him." I could hear Ms. Poke failed attempt to whisper as I strolled off.

"Poke, be quiet girl. You don't know dat girl. And you don't know what dat boy is going through."

Chapter 46: Flex's Prodigy
Scene: West Charity Street

I don't know a single person that owned a Rolls Royce. It was hard to get a look at the driver through the presidential tint. I wondered who the fuck it was that was bold enough to come through here in some shit like that and not show face. Mother fucker lucky I ain't flip that bitch upside down. Hopefully, the driver was lost and just passing by. "Aye Flex! What's up big dawg." My attention was distracted by my little nigga Wolf. He was crossing the street approaching me. Little nigga looked fucked up. Shoes dirty, clothes dusty. His head was beanie as a bitch.

"Wats up lil nigga? Why are you looking so fucked up?"

"Shidd nigga, you been missing in action. Without you, it's been hard to eat out dis bitch. Block hot as a bitch. 12 been lockin niggas up left and right. Killing and all types of shit. Niggas scared to come out dis bitch. Ain't no work."

"Maine look," I had to cut the little dude off. Fuck the past. I know how fucked up shit was. Shit, I'm the one that fucked it up. But now I'm about to fuck it up. "Don't trip bout none of dat shit. If you are rocking with me, you're going to be straight. Ion give a fuck bout dem other niggas. Fuck da opps."

"Speaking of da opps. I think dem TNH niggas up da street plotting to bring you a move right now. That's how I know dat you were right here."

"Dem niggas can pull up if dey want. Dey ass gone put down."

"Q!" It was Pam coming from down the street. She had more energy than she had earlier. She also had a few people with her. I knew I could count on her. Too bad she couldn't say the same for me. "Here he go y'all. I'm tellin' you too, that's da shit from da summer."

I made the first play for a hundred dollars before handing the pack over to Wolf. "Dime fo dime, "I told him.

"No deals. No shorts." Wolf caught the plays and passed the test by handing the money over to me.

"Wat bout me Flex?" Pam asked in confusion mixed with impatience.

"Didn't I already look out for you Pam?"

"Yeah, but.." she had a dumbfounded look on her face. "I thought dat was a tester."

"Look at it like a two-for-one deal." Pam sucked her teeth.

"Oh my God. I fuckin hate you! I swear I wish Q was here" She expressed, depressed while stomping off.

"Oh well." I shrugged my shoulders. Bitch better kick rocks. I was gone smack the shit out of her if she didn't. As Pam dragged her feet across the street, a Range Rover was turning into the projects on the street I stood on. I was sure that this was Streets. It was his car, and I could clearly see him through the window. I threw up my arms looking for an encounter as he rolled past. That nigga tapped the horn and kept it pushing. I wasn't going to be that easily denied. Streets were the plug that I needed to elevate my hustle. I mean, I already had about four bricks, but was in fear of what I would do if I was to run out other than all the bullshit. That was another reason why I wasn't in full gear in hustle mode. "Aye, you strapped right?" I asked Wolf.

"You already know, fool."

"Good, let's go see what's going on up da street. It's one too many foreigners riding through this bitch, and ain't none of dem mine."

Chapter 47: Dawn's Diary
Scene: Her Crib

A rhythm of knocks was striking my front door. It kind of pissed me off because I had just tuned into my studies. The college warned me that the final decision could take days or even months. I was ready to claim it as if it had already manifested. At the same time though, no one ever approached this door. I was curious as to who decided to pay me a visit. I got up off the couch, pulled up my ping boy shorts out of the crack of my ass and headed to the door. Looking through the peephole, it was hard to make out the face. All I noticed was a muscular man with braids. "Who is it?" I asked agitated.

"It's me."

"It's me?" I whispered to myself. Who the fuck had the nerve. "Who da fuck is me?" I yelled through the door, turning up my attitude which wasn't good at all. I really started to boil when whoever me was refused to answer me. I left 'me' to stand on the other side of the door looking stupid. I headed to the back to snatch up my snub nose .380 revolver. Well, technically, Q had left it here a long time ago, but it was mine now. I pulled the door open in haste with my left hand and grasped the pistol in the right. With the barrier of the closed door now removed, I was able to stand face-to-face with the knocker. My lungs stopped pumping. He took the air out of me. Then my heart stopped beating. He took that as well. As soon as my intellect registered the fact that it was Q, I lost consciousness.

"You right?" Are you back now?" The sweet sound of his voice circulated to the drum of my ears. It was like music from Heaven. How was this possible?

"What happened?" Was all I was able to utter, not really knowing exactly what I was questioning about. All I knew was that my life went blank from bafflement. Now I was laid out on my own couch with my head laid on a pillow that rested in his lap. I looked up at him. He was looking down at me while running his finger through the loose strings of my hair. I looked into his eyes and relaxed as my lack of conviction was washed away. Felicity. I haven't felt this good since .. since Q.

"Well, first, I thought you were ready to shoot me. Cause I know yo ass fuckin crazy." I laughed at his comment. He had a real gift of being amusing during a serious moment of dialog. I think that's how he got me to open in the first place. It was either that or those fucking eyes. I would include the dick game, but truth be told, I was already gone before that. "Then I realized da you had my gun in yo hand dat I used in dat shootout. I guess you ain't know it, but da shit is still empty. The next thing I knew, you were collapsing to da floor. I just picked you up, laid you on da couch, and placed an ice-cold rag on yo forehead. You still had a pulse and were still breathing. So, I just waited for you to wake up." I felt stupid about the empty gun part. Do you know how long I thought that gun was gone protect me? I never thought to check the chamber. "You know," Q continued, "Da whole time, I sat right here trying to figure out what was going through your mind while you were unconscious cause your nipples were hard da whole time."

I sucked my teeth. "Boy." And reached up to smack him in his face. Playfully though. His smile gleamed like the rays of the rising sun. "It's cold in here." I lied. Playfully again though.

"No, it's not." He exposed my lie. "Keep it real." He played the game right along with me. "You were thinking about me, weren't you?"

I giggled. "Ion know what I was thinking about. I was un-conscious."

"You know dey say when you're unconscious, that's when you really find your true self?"

"Oh yea? Well, who said dat?"

"Ion know. That's just wat they say. What's up with dis lil pink book right here though?" I sensed that he was either trying to change the subject or very unduly curious about my diary that he now held in hand.

I sucked my teeth again. "Boy! You know what da fuck dat is."

"I'm just saying, it must be one real top-secret shit in here. You got da lil lock on dis bitch and everything."

"If you want to read it Q, all you have to do is ask."

"What do I look like? A privacy invader." I stared up at him with a look of 'really' on my face. "Ight, ight, ight, ight. I just want to see wat you were going through for da past few... Fo da time I was gone." Speaking of him being gone, where da fuck has he been?

"You can just ask me Q."

"Yeaaa.. but I'd much rather just sum it all up. Besides, when you wrote da words on des pages, it was motivated by da original feelings of that moment. Right?" I agreed with him but didn't say it. I removed the dairy from his hand. The dairy came with a secret compartment for the key underneath the furry cover that covered the cover. "Wat da fuck?" Q asked under his breath.

"What?" I asked while unlocking the dairy.

"Sometimes you think you have seen it all. I guess you never know." I don't know what the fuck Q was talking about. He was acting stranger than the day I first met him. I handed him the open diary and allowed him to read. I waited quietly as he flipped through the pages reading the words of my heart.

"So, you started a dairy on da day I got shot?" He asked a very obvious question.

"Yes, Q," I answered anyway. "I needed a way to express my feelings. I found dat placing them on paper was a great relief."

"So, did it stop you from having da thoughts of killin' yo self? I sighed. "Yes, Q."

"What about my baby?"

"I never was going to kill myself or OUR baby. They were just thoughts."

"Well, thoughts are like seeds. Seeds are jus seeds till they grow into a forest of trees."

"And what are you, a squirrel?"

"Yes, just looking for a nut." We both laughed out loud. See what I mean? I couldn't take him for a joke. But was on edge about taking him seriously.

"I fuckin' hate you."

"We ain't gone do dat."

"Do what?"

"Dat was a second lie you told me in twenty minutes, and you were passed out fo 15 of dem."

"I'm only joking with you Q. What, you can joke but I can't?"

"Ain't no lies in my jokes. Just the truth. Besides, it's a difference between joking and lying."

"Boy! Whatever! Wat are you all of a sudden, a philosopher?"

"You can be whatever you wanna be Q. Long as you be it with me." I had zoned out looking towards the ceiling but not really looking at it. I was absorbing this wonderful feeling I experienced now, while visualizing the future. This morning I woke up gloomy, fighting with all my might to push myself through this cloudy day. Never in a million years would I expect Q to pop up at my doorstep. This was a one-in-a-million probability. I really didn't pay attention to how quiet Q was. Until he was no longer quiet anymore.

"Wat da fuck is Flex doing in yo diary?" Looking back at Q, he held a perplex perilous expression on his face. No sign of jest was detected.

"Well Q, if you read it, you'll find out. Because obviously you didn't." He took some time to read over the page with the head titled Flex. I assumed he read it twice because it shouldn't have taken that long. It was only a page.

"Did he say anything about me?" He asked after dropping the book.

"No. He was jus thirsty and tryina fuck." I could tell that pissed Q off. "Does he know dat I'm pregnant? With yo seed?"

"Naw, I ain't tell nobody. Only way somebody knows if you told'em."

"Well, I didn't."

"Good. Don't. And get rid of dis diary. You don't need it now."

"Huh!?" I asked like a little girl being placed on punishment for something she really didn't do. "Fo wat Q? I like my diary."

"Fo one, cause I said so. And fo two cause you saying too much in dis book. Dis shit full of conspiracy theories." I've seen Q very serious at times, but never this stern.

"Ok, I will."

"Naw, you ain't got to. I will."

"So, why don't you want people to know about da baby?"

"Cause it ain't dey business. And it's other shit dat's going on dat I need to clean up. I have to make sure I keep you and my seed safe. But there is one person Ima have to tell though."

"Who is dat?"

"Keyshia. My baby's momma." I already knew that. Just wanted to see what he would say since he is talking about being honest.

"So, when you gone tell me wat happened?"

"Wit wat?"

"Q don't play stupid. I thought you were dead. And again, here you are in my presence."

"Well, I'm not dead. Don't make it seem like such a bad thing."

"It's not a bad thing, far from it. I'm just sick of having dis fear of losing you. All these disappearing acts are gettin' tiring Q. You gotta bitch goin' through depression, anxiety, and God knows wat other mental health issues." I felt it coming on again just at the mention of the mixed emotions. I used both of my hands to cover my face. The last thing I wanted was for him to watch me cry on the happiest day of my life. I felt his hands wrap around both of my wrists. He uncovered my face and we locked eyes.

"Listen Dawn, Ima say dis wit out soundin' too harsh. You gone have to get ova dat fear of losin' me. I say dat cause you'll never lose me. Even if you do so physically, I'll always be connected to you. Trust me on dis. As far as all yo other worries, I'm here now and to my best abilities, Ima do whatever possible to help you ease those pains. Sometimes I may not be able to expose everything. Just know dat I'll never mislead you. If you follow my lead, I'll guide you in da right direction. Do you understand?" I didn't say a word. But I did nod my head yes.

"I just need you here Q."

"Do you not have me here? I'm right here. Jus focus on da here, da now." For wat seemed like an eternity, our souls sparkled through our eyes. He leaned in and placed his lips on mine. They were so soft and warm. Instantly, I slid my tongue into his mouth. Now our tongues danced in a sensuous rhythm. He used his hand and slid it into my penniless boy shorts. To say that my lips down low were wet would be a minor understatement. Let's say soaked. He gently rubbed his palm over my freshly shaved cat. Then used two fingers to separate my pussy lips in search of my throbbing clitoris. Once he discovered the buried jewel, he flickered at it sending tingling vibes up my spine. It's been so long, so many long, lonely nights, sleeping with an urge that I can only crave for him to fulfill. He took his other hand and used it to rub my breast through the wife beater I wore. As if the level of pleasure I was already in wasn't enough. It caused me to release a moan. I wanted to release all the frustrations that were locked inside this trembling body of mine.

I got up and removed the pillow from his lap. I replaced the pillow with my ass which was probably softer anyway. I aggressively pulled the sweatshirt over his head and tossed it on the couch. His torso was so ripped and toned with defined muscles. I wanted to see it all. I poked a hole in his white wife beater and ripped it open exposing his chest and ice tray six-pack. I rubbed my fingernails down his chest and cut abs causing him to shiver. He grabbed my ass and gripped it with purpose. Rubbing both of my cheeks in an up-down motion.

I couldn't take it anymore. I stood and slid the pinks off. I loved the way he admired my whole body from my eyes to my toes. I yanked the sweatpants from around his waist and everything else that was concealing his symbol of manhood. Once exposed, I did some admiring myself. I stood up strong and firm. Climbing back on top of Q, I wrapped my hands around his neck. Looking deeply into his eyes, I found the tip of his dick with my pussy. Slowly, I wiggled and whined my walls around his pole. It feels so good that it caused me to purr. It's been so long, it almost felt like the first time. One that made it better though was the experience. That and the mixture of passion and love. My pussy was so tight. His dick was so hard. The juices that dripped made it easier for the activities of our private parts to collaborate. Stirring my emotions like the waves of the ocean, I leaned in to kiss Q more. He was a wonderful kisser. He also knew where to put his hands at the right times. Right now, he was rubbing them down my back as I straddled his saddle in a slow and steady motion. Up, down, back, and forth. His hands rested on the small of my back where my pierced dimples were. He played with the dimple rings before sliding his hands back down to my ass cheeks. He found the crack of my ass and slid a couple of fingers down until they found the bottom of my pussy where his dick entered. He played with the area, rubbing, and tapping it. I arched my back as I leaned in closer to Q resting my breast on his chest. He buried his face in my neck and bit, licked, and intensified the rhythm by pumping his dick into me. "Yes Q. Fuck me. Fuck me good." I begged in his ear, before biting the lope of it.

Q used his other hand and rubbed his fingers around my anal area. It tickled and elevated the pleasure. Unexpectedly, he had slid the tip of one of his fingers into my ass hole. Caught off guard, I was shocked and surprised. He pulled the finger out, rubbed the anal some more, and slid it in again. Somehow, it caused the muscles in my pussy to contract, squeezing my walls around Q's murder weapon as he killed my pussy. "Oh my God ... Yes! Yes!" I felt whole and complete. My wish was to remain in this moment for life. Each second was meaningful, making me mindful of the mystical mysteries unknown.

I rode Q's dick as if I was competing in the Kentucky Derby. He tapped my ass as you would a horse begging it to get up. My cheeks loudly clapped into his lap. Splashing in the puddle of fluids our bodies created, I swallowed his whole dick up with my pussy all down to his balls. I'd put them in if I could. I wanted all of him. My eyes were rolling in the back of my head. My tongue spoke a language of its own. "I 'cha I. Uh, tis, tis, cee." My legs shook as my toes curled. I knew what would happen next, so I braced for it. I wrapped my hands around Q's throat and choked him. I wanted to make him mad. Piss him off. I wanted him to fuck me with everything he had.

"Bitch!" He said in a raspy voice. Ima let that one slide. It worked but I wanted more. Still choking, I planted kisses on his lips. He fell for the trick trying to kiss me back as best as he could. I sucked his bottom lip into my mouth and bit it, holding his lip in between my teeth. Now, I knew he was mad. He grabbed the back of my neck and squeezed it. He took his other hand and grabbed a handful of my hair. He wrapped it around his hand until he was able to have a locking grip. Together we focused all of our pain, frustration, and pleasure towards our sexual organs. Focusing on my g-spot, I rocked on his dick until my body tapped out. The heaven gates were open allowing juices, ecstasy, and life to flow through my body. I collapsed from weakness. I could no longer ride.

Q wasn't finished though. He put his hands underneath my thighs from my front. He locked his arms into my legs, folding my body with my knees to my breast. He was so strong that it was heating me up again. With his own strength and ambition, he controlled my whole body by sliding me up and on his dick. I held on to his shoulders for balance. He multi-tasked by controlling himself and me. Soon he was bursting into me like a star. I wrapped my arms around him and him as tight as I could. I missed him so much. I didn't want to let him go. I was too deep in love.

Chapter 48: Flex Faults
Scene: St. Paul Street

By the time Wolf and I had made it up Saint Paul Street, I spotted Street's Rover parked. It was damn near in the same spot where I killed Q and them two pigs. I knew Streets was still in the car because it was surrounded by a group of niggas that probably had the same intention as me.

The presence of Streets had brung the hood out. It was just dry as solid carbon dioxide out here. Reggie stood off at a distance alongside Big Dee. "Wats up bad azz? Big Dee, wats good?" I greeted closing the distance between the two.

"Ayee wats up lil nigga?" Reggie replied calmly. I could tell that he was playing it cool. I didn't forget about earlier. Despite the friction, we dapped up and lightly embraced.

"Aye Flex, wats good fool?" Big Dee now spoke. "Wats up wit all dat money you owe me from dem packs we rushed? I know you got yo lil shit going on, but ion respect da fact you just up and left a nigga hanging out to dry like dat. Nigga got bills to pay. Kids to feed." I understood where Big Dee was coming from. That doesn't necessarily mean that I gave a fuck. He was expressing a lot of problems that weren't mine. But still, though, I could use this situation for the benefit of my plans to come.

I usually don't do shit like this, ever. I reached into my pockets and peeled off a handful of bills. I ain't even bother to count it. Just acted like I did. "My bad fool." I handed the money over to Big Dee. "I was gone get ya'll niggas straight. Just was waiting for shit to cool down some." I lied with ease. In the mix of denying my faults. I was peeling off some money to hand to Reggie as well. I definitely had to keep that nigga off my line. Plus, both of these niggas would be important pieces on the chess board later on in the game.

"So, wats up wit dat mission from earlier? Everything went smooth?" Reggie asked.

"Huh?" I was almost confused.

"Da drill nigga?"

"Oh yeah Maine, bitch ass nigga got away. I'ma catch another drop though. Shit ain't bout none fr."

"I see you got yo lil stick partner wit you." Reggie referred to Wolf standing in my shadow.

"Yeah Maine." Was all I said quickly changing subjects. "Ayee, wats up wit dem niggas?" I nodded my head towards the crowd gathered around Street's car.

"Shidd, you know how it is when Streets pull up. I'm surprised he's been out here for dis long."

"No bullshit." Big Dee agreed with Reggie. "On some real shit though, I ain't seen 12 out dis bitch like all day."

"Dem bitches probably scared to death or plotting. Guess yo reckless ass plan worked out Flex." Reggie said.

"Wat plan?" Reggie, Big Dee, and Wolf looked at me as if I was senile. "Oh yeah. I told ya'll niggas all we had to do was put pressure on dem crackas. Dem ma'fuckas ain't tryna die just like we ain't." For real though, I thought Reggie was talking about some shit that he wasn't supposed to know. "I'ma catch up with ya'll niggas later though. Come on Wolf."

"Where da hell are you going now?" asked Reggie.

"I gotta holla at Streets about some real business. Dem niggas ova der ain't talking about shit. Probably beggin'."

"Ion think you should go ova der fuckin with dem niggas right now Flex." Reggie advised. "I told you niggas still salty bout Burga, and a lot of other shit if you wanna be a hunnit."

"And I already told you fuck 'em. Dem niggas ain't gone do shit. Wolf, let's go!"

"Ight." Reggie's last words were bouncing off my back. I was already headed towards my destination. When I pulled up, Hawk was leaning into the passenger window of Street's car. He stood up straight when he noticed me walking up.

"Look who back ya'll." Hawk entertained the crowd. I ain't gone lie, I knew a day would come when he and I would have to go toe to toe. Today may be that day. I wasn't talking about a boxing match either.

166

"Streets, wats up big dawg?" I ignored Hawk and leaned in to get a view of Streets in the car. "Ayee, let me holla at you right quick." I don't know if I was tripping, but I could have sworn that I was picking up on a vibe change. His expression turned frosty as if he had no rap for a nigga. If that hypothesis was accurate, then I would conclude that it probably came from all that shit he heard about me in recent times. It was cool though. All I needed was a chance to dialog and I would change his whole point of view.

"Damn nigga! Don't up see niggas talking?" spat Hawk

I was ready to kill this nigga. I'm talking about right now in front of everybody. I ain't even give a fuck no more. Then it hit me. I never gave a fuck. Then it hit me again, I had the policy under my foot and won't take advantage of this hit.

I tugged at the Glock .40 under my belt. The gun got caught in my boxers forcing me to take another draw attempt. By that time, Hawk had gained a step up on me standing with his pistol in hand and everyone else including Wolf and myself, with pistols Clutch, positioned ourselves for a standoff. Reggie and Big Dee were jogging from their posted spot toward the crowd. Simultaneously, streets was climbing out of his car and walking towards the other side

"Aye wats up with niggas? We're ready to die out dis bitch or wat?" Reggie asked unflinchingly, building his way into the middle of the crowd.

"Maine yall lil' crazy ma'fuckers put des guns up before yall made dis shit hot out here" Streets ordered. No one obeyed, I knew that whoever shot first or whenever the first shot went off, it would set off a chain reaction of flying bullets. I definitely had plans of being the cause of that first shot being fired. The only thing is that my shit wasn't clear enough yet. I attempted to go unnoticed as I took small steps backwards. I'll be dumb ass fuck to get caught dead in the crossfires.

"Ayee Streets, go ahead and get back in the car big bruh, you ain't got none to do wit dis"

Yeah, but I'on want none of yall niggas to do none stupid. Ain't enough of yall niggas died already? Wat bout da agreement we made in unity?" Street stood firm in the middle of the crowd.

Dat was some shit Q put us up to. Dis nigga, ain't none like Q." Hawk lifted his gun and pointed it at me.

"Yeah, but dis still his brother though a fool."Reggie verbalized.

'Ion give a fuck bout none of dat shit." Hawk stated angrily. Streets had got a ring from his phone causing him to put his head down while digging into his pockets. I hurriedly upped my pistol taking advantage of the clear shot at Hawk. BOOM!BOOM! Both shots zoomed past Street's head barely missing him. They missed Hawk by a longshot. One bullet slammed into the face of a person standing right behind him. I rarely ever missed my target this close. Then again, I never had to deal with so many nigga staying to block my shots. Regardless of all that other shit, I was now ducking and dodging bullets. Bodies scattered. Some fell. It was hard to tell who was aiming for who. We all shot with the intent to kill for no purpose. Well, I had a purpose. It was to reign. So logically, the opps purpose was to stop me. Couldn't we find another way to dispute over difficulties? Nope! I let off a chain of shots hoping to make anyone of these niggas think twice before aiming my way. A few of my shots found the torso of a nigga who had his back turned. He had no sense of direction and now his nobody fell in on-direction. Now was down to the ground smacking the pavement like a spaldon.

"Aww, shit! Bitch!" They say when Karma goes around, it has to come back. One of these nigga hit me in my right triceps. I grabbed the back of my arm with my left hand to keep it steady. Spinning around, I let off shots at any and everybody in the way to catch them. Now, from the opposite direction, the opposition sent a shot to the back of my head "Fuck" I got low and duck-walked to the side of street car. Ping, Ping, Ping! As soon as I got my back settled on the backend of the car, bullets were penetrating the body of the vehicle. I was on the move again creeping around the driver's side of the car. I popped up and settled my gun on the roof. With both hands, I took aim at targets. BANG!BANG! Two to the temple of a target that took aim at Wolf. In return, Wolf clipped another nigga who I overlooked. He was able to get one shot off before one shot to his throat caused him to take his last breath. The force of gravity laid his body down vigorously. I scanned the field for Hawk. He was hard to find. Instead, I found Big Dee and Reggie back to back keeping each other breathing. I spotted Red and Blu ducked behind a wall in the hallway, down the street. Niggas were everywhere purging, thugging like it was legal. Is this what I really wanted? All I wanted was for niggas to do as I say. Was that so hard to do?

I had a call coming in on my phone. Not my phone but that phone. You know, the phone I got from Lil shawty. Really? Like right now? I thought to myself. Hiding behind the car again, I answered the phone because I knew that it had to be urgent, plus, that was her order. Ain't that a bitch? Look at me! Willing to take orders from the police" Hello" I answered.

I don't know what da hell yall got going on there. But you need to leave. And fast. I tried to catch da calls but it's so many of dem coming in. A few of them passed our system. They are in pursuit as we speak."

"Say no more" I hung the phone up and searched for my escape route. Oh yeah, here we go. I yanked open the driver's door to the Range Rover, only to find streets stuck in the driver's seat, His body was held up by the support of the headrest. He was closed as if he was in a deep peaceful meditative state. I knew better. Another soul was lost in the streets at the expense of another. I closed the door, stood up, and upped my gun. As I pulled the trigger, the firing pin sparked allowing bullets to be freed from its chamber. I shot at nobody in particular. Just trying to make a way for my exit. I sprinted up Q back which would land me on Saint John Street. Ducking as bullets followed me, I still had spots on O block; that was my destination. While ramming down John, I noted the Rolls Royce that rolled through earlier, parked. To King Q's mental note, I kept strolling. Had to cluck the rollers.

Chapter 49: Q's Quality
Scene: Dawn's Crib

My eyes were damn near rolled in the back of my head. The tip of my dick was deep down Dawn's throat. She harmonized on it, sending vibrated tingles throughout my shoulder. I don't think there was anything that could snatch me out of this delighted moment.

BOOM!BOOM!BOOM! Dawn lifted her head in freight. Same old shit I see. She got up off her knees and climbed onto the couch. His naked smoothed skin body crawled underneath mine. "I'm so sick of dis shit" she laid her head on my shoulder. Dis shit I like everyday round here. Den it's always round dis building dat makes it worse. Police kill in niggas. Niggas killing police. Kids getting killed just for playing. While clothes are being dragged into the war. It seemed like a lil while da killings had slowed down. But I guess that was wishful thinking."

"Where da money dat I gave you?"

I still have it. I haven't spent a dime."

"Why didn't you get from 'round here?"

I was saving so I could re-enter college. Da rest would be used for our seed."

"Go get it and whatever other lil items you need to take with you. "No questions asked, she went out and did as I asked her. I threw my clothes back on and packed her laptop and books into a book bag that sat on the floor beside the table. Dawn came back fully dressed and ready to go. "You got yo key?"

"Yelp," she confirmed, holding them up for me to see.

"Let's go." We left out the front door, traveled down the stairs and headed up the front towards St. John Street. As I spoke at this very moment, a battle of bullets were taking place on the other side of the block. Dawn and I jogged to the car, hopped in, and sped away in the smooth ride of the Rolls Royce.

"Q, who's car is dis?" Dawn was in amazement. She looked and felt around the car as if she was experiencing a whole new world.

"It's ours," I told her. "But you better not get my ears wet," she giggled at my response but remained speechless for the duration of the ride. That was fine with me. I needed the time to think anyway. Back to the basics again I guess. One thing I knew about Q, is when he was at his best. Speaking in third person of course. Besides, before you got to the cap, you had to establish the cornerstones.

I pulled up by the Fountain Fortune Apartments. I don't know if you remember but I literally helped build this complex of condos from the ground up. Long story made short, this was the place where streets had granted me first place of employment. Now a number of beautiful buildings stood six stories high. Parking in front of the kind Lord's rental office, I told Dawn to grab the bag full of money and to come with me. Together, we walked through the doors of the office and headed over to the receptionist standing behind the desk. "Good evening Lady and Gentleman. Welcome to the Fountain Fortune apartments. How may I assist you?"

"How are you doing? We are well. Just looking for a place to leash."

"Ok well, that's not a problem at all. You've wisely come to the right place. I can get you started right away. First, you'll need two forms of identification proof of income, and down payment for the first three-month rent, which will vary depending on the state of placement.. The problem is that I had no means of Identification and no proof of income. All I had was enough money to pay rent in advance for years for the best apartment available. "And while you gather your needed information, could you give me the name of the head of the house that will be placed at the top of the leash?' I thought about Dawn who stood by my side. Making her the head of the whole house would guarantee us the apartment. But it wasn't secure for me to go about it that way. I mean yeah, she had thought a few things with me. Some even begin life or death. But could I depend on her to be loyal until the end? I've seen her lose her control due to her bi-polar disorder and completely flip on me. Who's to say that she wouldn't do it again in the future and try to put me out on my ass when I made a move that she disagreed with? I'd rather take a chance on myself. Besides, who in the world would turn down this money because of lack of I.D,

"Andreson. Dequan Anderson."

"Ok, Mr. DaQuan." the receptionist started typing on a desktop computer" Anderson. The expression on her pale face turned blushed. She picked up the receiver of the phone. "I have a J-13 here. Yes. Ok. The phone call ended. "Umm Mr. Anderson, I surely do give my apologies. Someone will be down in the next minute to show you up." I'm not sure what she was sorry for. She was nothing but nice and respectful since I stepped through these doors. Now, all of a sudden, there seemed to be no need for all the documents that were just required. Even my money was no longer wanted. You think I'm complaining about any of it? Not at all.

Dawn and I walked across the lobby to take an ascent while we waited. "What was all dat bout?" Dawn asked, clearly confused.

"I'on know' wats going on" I played as dumb ass possible. Moments later, a tall Caucasian man was coming from the back of the office. Upon his entrance through the door seal, I caught the emotion of a sign he displayed with his hands. I also caught the fact that the receptionist threw one back. The signs were familiar to me now. They were some of the same ones I saw back at lodge of the lost cultivated society. To the naked eye, it may seem as if a person was doing regular gestures. Like scratching or rubbing a certain spot of the body a certain way. One thing that I was completely sure of was that it all went way over Dawn's head. She was blind to the very things that took place directly in her face.

"Mr. Anderson," the tall man called me over" You and your friend, right his way please sir. "Without saying a word, I got up and Dawn followed. We were led to the bank where the tall gentleman had just appeared emo. We all entered an elevator and went up all the way up to the top floor. The elevator stopped but the doors didn't open, the aristocrat pulled out a key card and scanned it causing a small red light to turn green. The moment the green light flashed, the doors were open, welcoming us directly to the master suite.

The inside was up-scale, fully furnished with confrontation, and fastened with fascinating structure. It held their bedrooms and both had their own bathrooms. A beautiful spacious kitchen with all the appliances and some, of course, a living room, where an IV hung from the wall, the size of a projector scene. A balcony and another door attached to the balcony that led to the rooftop of the building on the rooftop was a pool surrounded by many beach chairs. There was a fireplace sticking out of the ground which supported a bar and a place for serving food. The view over the top of the complex was what really had my attention. Felt like I was on top of the world. I only dreamed of being able to live in a place such as this. I guess dreams do come true. Dawn wasn't too flabbergasted herself. Although, I could tell that she was grateful to be out of other projects and ready to get comfortable. That's one thing I like about Dawn, although she lived in the projects, she always kept her dealings classy, even down to her occupation. She was the most sophisticated stripper I had ever met in my life. "Mr. Andeson, could I have a word with you in private please sir?"

"Sure," I said before asking Dawn to leave us to be on the rooftop alone.

"You do know that we have obligations to fulfill to you right my brother?" The man's whole demeanor changed. It went from polite to eagerly serious. This is one of our fulfillments. Your livelihood is very important to our families' society. In return, when your time comes, you will also be called upon to fulfill your duties as well. Think nothing of it for we are more than happy to welcome you. You have made it through things that most men die from. You deserve to live in abundance. The work is only beginning. Just be ready. Enjoy your stay and be on the lookout for brother Tyson Carter. He will be in touch with you soon. If you ever need me, I'm literally one call away. Just like that. Without even giving me a chance to ask a question, or even say thank you to the mystery man; he was making his way out of my sight.

Dawn and I showered. Immediately after drying off, we realized that neither of us had fresh clothes to put on. She damn near cursed me out when I suggested that we put our dirty clothes back on. It was either that or I would leave her ass here because I was about to hit the road. Like I thought, she did as I did. Our first stop was the mall. We blew a bag on us and our unborn. We were so pressed for time that we changed our clothes right there in the mall. She was Chanel down, from her earrings to her heels. I walked out rocking an off-white outfit with a pair of regular all-white air Forces. You know I'ma keep-it-simple type of nigga. To cover up the naps that remain on my head, I topped the fit off with a jean denim Miami Heat new era fitted from Lids. Before exiting the mall, we zapped by the food court to grab some things to eat. She wanted Jamaica. I want Chinese. I had also snatched up a phone. Well, actually two. It was hard for me to choose between the new iPhone or the new Galaxy, which is always my favorite.

On our next stop, Dawn and I swung by the Richmond City Jail. You don't have to say it. I already know what you are thinking. Like why? I agree. But we were on the juvenile wing. Plus, I basically had a get-out-of-jail-free card. Come on, you know that the fuck going on. Stop acting like you ain't been keeping up with the story. Anyway, I had to check up on one of my youngins, Jay Jr. All I Know is that he was being held here because he was being charged as an adult. I had to check in as his visitor. I was just an anonymous associate. Jay Jr. was happy as hell to see Dawn pop up on the visitor scene. He popped a lot of shit trying his best to bag her. I know the young had a thing for her. Shit, what nigga wouldn't? Dawn just laughed the whole visit getting a major kick out of the kid.

My first intention was to holla at Jay Jr. myself. Then my intuition kicked in. I don't think that would've been the smartest thing to do. Instead, I sat off to the side where I could clearly view him on the scene but out of the camera's sight. He had no idea that I was ever there. I had got what I came for. I needed to know the status of his case. Basically, the Prosecutor was trying to drag out the trial in order to buy time for more evidence. All they had was the testimony of the officer. However, those were the words of the same police that shot Young G. Speaking of Young-G, I had also found out from listening to Jay Jr. that he had made it out of the hospital after being on life support for a while now. He was ducked off somewhere living with his grandmother. After the visit with Jay Jr., I let Dawn climb behind the heel of the double R. She was more thrilled than a child on Christmas morning. I directed her to head to VCU Campus. At this point when it came to Dawn, all I Had to do was say so, and she would make it happen. Surely, I had made her a believer of my qualities. She did whatever she had to do once we pulled up onto the campus. I remained in the car. As I waited, I saw this fine-ass brown sugar complexion chick with olive green eyes and a pair of thick-ass lips walking by the car. Being that I wanted to feel the brisk breeze of the Mid-November weather, I didn't see any harm in dropping my window. I wouldn't think that this would be a place where anyone would know me from a can of paint. For some reasons though, the way Lil Shawty was eyeing a nigga as he walked by was something else. I may have to beg to differ. Either I looked oddly familiar to her or she just wanted me to fuck the shit out of her in the back of the Rolls Royce. It was hard to tell which one, maybe it was both. Who knows.

Spotting Dawn heading out of the building, I politely rolled the window up. Using the tints to black my view from the little thirst bucket. Like I said though, Lil Shawty was bad. Right now though, I had too much respect for my baby momma; she was heading too far in the right direction of me to risk it all for a nut.

Dawn climbed into the car almost a little too enthused.' Oh my God Q! I love you so much! Thank you!" she squealed in a high-pitched voice while reaching over to give me a hug. "I owe you so much for dis. I swear I will make it up to you."

"Dawn, you don't owe me any of this. Except one thing."

"Ok, and wats dat? I don't care what it is. With me, your wish is my command."

"Succeed. Dats it just succeed."

"I got you baby daddy!" She said with exciting sarcasm.

Chapter 50
Q's Closed Mouth Gathering

Scene! Secretive
6 Months Later

"We gathered her in secrecy to celebrate the elevations of Jeremiah 13's degrees within our brotherhood. Jeremiah 13, within the last six months, you have ascended and raised it to higher levels quicker than a lot of four recent apprentices. In fact, the most recent member to have climbed up the stairs of our way of life as speedy as you were other than your father. You have obeyed all rules and fulfilled all obligations when called upon. In addition, you have also found great success for yourself. Reconnecting back with our very own, Mr. Tyson Carter, you were willing to re-establish your work relations. By means of hard work, you were able to make a business corporation cut off employment. Now, not only do you have a contract in the garbage department with so many dump trucks, but you also own a percentage of "From the Ground Up Construction"

Proud is not a word powerful enough to explain how excited I am for you. Your future is looking so bright. Also, word has reached me from the Mayor's Office that you are looking into investing in red zone properties. I will do my part by giving a good word on your behalf to see that your wish is granted. My only wish is that you remain straight on your travel to greatness. Let us make a toast" Finally, Supreme was done with another of the long-winded speeches. We all raised our glasses, clinked them into one another, and took sips from our cups. I tilted my cup all the way until the bottom was up.

These past six months have been tiring. In the eyes of someone looking in, it may have seemed highly successful, which it was. What they couldn't see was the hard work that was put into the find. The sacrifices made in order to take another step ahead. The losses. The loss of sleep. Lost time. Lost of happiness I know right? Stop bitching. Man up. Your ight.

Still, to this day, I moved as if I was dead to the streets. Like a ghost. That was a sacrifice within itself. So you know how badly I wanted to pop out? How badly I wanted to prove to all my doubters that I was a true survivor. Not only a survivor but a success as well. I thought plenty of times to myself, what sense did it make to win if I couldn't see the looks on my competitors' faces when they lost? Oh and flex, I couldn't wait to see the look on that nigga face. Even if I really was dead, I would've made it my business to hang that bitch down every night in his dreams like Freedy, wake him up and kill his ass again.

Pretty sure you know already but I lost my mentor. My plug, the person I felt like I could trust in this word. Yeah, Streets was gone. I don't even know how to feel about it. To be honest, I felt this life-changing me. I felt my emotions shut down. My heart is freezing over. There seems to be nothing or anyone I cared for anymore other than me. Felt like people never really cared for me. Just what I could do for them. It was hard to identify with myself any longer. After six months on top of all those other months, I have yet to see my daughters. It's been a year now. At first, I searched hard for their location. As time went on, I found myself being more engaged in my work. Before I knew it, my search was halted. Plus, I was having second thoughts on this society shit. I mean niggas were cool. I felt as if I could get any and everything I wanted. But for some strange reason, I was starting to lose value in myself.

Would I have been this successful if it wasn't for the helping hand of the society? The whole time I was fooled to think that I was doing it all on my own. Was I really? Back when Streets gave me that chance, was that a plan, or a test? I put in the work at the job. Got rid of the work on the block, and did right by the money. But still though, as a matter of fact, was I forgetting about the grave? I made it out of that bitch by the grave of my brave heart. What the fuck is it I'm talking about? I deserve everything I got and all that is coming. Good or bad. So you get what I'm saying though? The confusion.

There was at least one thing I was sure about though. That was the love that I have for my newborn son. He was literally the shine that I needed in my life at this moment. He was on his way to being three months old in about ten days. He was born a healthy chocolate little baby with a headful of hair. His birthday matched his personality perfectly. An April baby born on the first of the month; he was goofy as hell, playful, and very energetic. He is the closest thing to my heart these days. He played a big part in filling the void that I had from missing my daughters. I was also happy and proud of Dawn as well. With all the things she had going against her, she managed to finish up her courses. I could tell that she felt like a whole new woman. From a stripper to a lawyer. She definitely deserved to.

"Jeremiah 13, are you alright over there?" Supreme asked, breaking me out of my isolated state of mind while in a packed room full of people.

"Yeah. I'm good"

"Smile. It's a celebration."

"Yeah, you're right. Pass me da Ace. My cup is empty."

Self Made Tay

Chapter 51
Finally Flexing

Scene: Highway 64 East

Finally, shit was falling into place the way I planned. It took a while for a lot of nigga to get over some of the loses we took. But you know how the saying goes. Time heals all. Not to mention the problems that money could fix. I had everybody eating again. Even my opps. Yeah, you heard me right. I found out that success was the best killer. Them niggas hate the fact that they had to go through me in some type of way just to eat. It was a feeling that left me sickly satisfied. So satisfied that I figured, why kill them physically? Putting them out of their misery, when I could kill them financially? Making them my slaves.

Lil Shawty was highly on her shit too. She had recruited more loyal offices. Or should I say disloyal? I had the project on smash. Came to find out that the higher authority officials are as loving as the downward slope of the crime wave. Less bullets were flying, which meant less police and niggas were dying. Less niggas were hungry. So less niggas were forced to rob. To sum it all up, I guess you could say that less is more. More happy faces, more niggas staying in the place, more money for your boy. Life couldn't get any better for a nigga. Unless I could find a real plug.

Right now, I was dealing with niggas here and therefore, the right shit. It is always hit-and-miss. None of them were consistent. I was thinking about getting lil Shawty to try her hands in the evidence department. I'm pretty sure the precinct could be a hall of a plug for niggas. I really didn't want to risk what I already had going though. Having police being crooked on the streets was a big difference from having them do shit on the inside. Check me out though, thinking ahead and shit like that.

As of right now though, I won't think about shit but pick up speed. This nigga Wolf had just taken the lead on the open highway. I had brought five SRT DEMONS for my demons. We were putting every last one of them to use as we raced. 64 going

East. I pushed my demon to 120 mph breaking the tie with my yoga nigga Qua. He was a hell of a driver to be a Juvenile. But I was willing to put it all on the line. Caught up with Wolf coming within an inch of his bumper, I tried to sway right so I could go around him. He held the same though, cutting off my pathway. I switched back over to the left hoping that he would do the same. As expected, he did. With reckless speed, I shifted back over to the right and rushed to 125 mph. Got him, by now I was pulling up side by side with Wolf's all-black demon. He looked at me with a grin. I stuck my middle finger up at him and sped off slamming the pedal to the floor. I kept the lead all the way up until I slowed to shift over to the Nine Mile Road exit. The rest followed.

As I was getting off the highway. I noticed a Rolls Royce going in the opposite direction. It was the same one I remembered seeing parks around Jackson ward. We had a high roller ride right through this little small city of ours. I need to find out who the dude was. Maybe here would be the plug I was looking for all along. I pulled over to the Exxon and the other four cars pulled in right behind me. I stopped at a pump for a full-up. Across the pumps from us were five Trac Hawks. All of them were different shades of news. I was feeling they dropped to keep it real. I checked the license plates to find that they were visitors from the big State of Texas.

I guess I was staring a little too hard. The window of one of the Trac Hawks was dropping. You know I stayed strap, so was every nigga with me. I won't really trip at all, it was a bald-headed light skin nigga; he had tattoos over his head with light brown eyes. "Whoop. Sup blood? Tryna be where da homies at?"

"What's poppin' blood? Double I," I simply responded. I ain't gone lie to you, my city was really just getting on the blood wave. If you couldn't tell by now, I was on it. Red everything. I was also up there in the ranks too. Dude seems like a triple OG in the game though. Taking this shit a little too seriously. I mean, we stood on what we reaped but I guess things really were done bigger in Texas.

"212 Piru Blood. Pull up" I walked over to the car with Wolf and Blu who was actually blood himself. "Wat's up name youngin? I respected how do lil homies moving out here"

"Dey call me Flex."

He laughed "Ok. Flex huh? I like dat." He stuck his hand out the window to piece me up. "I'm Gotti Ru. Big Blood from Killeen Texas, I want you to take dis number. I might have some of' da homies before I head back deeper into da south."

"Ight bet" I said, growing anxious. "When should I hit yo line?"

"Anytime after today, blood down waits too late though. We'll be heading out soon."

"Say no more, I got you." I was turning to walk away.

"Ayee" Gotti Ru called out to me "Yall lil niggas slow dem demons down some. Gotta stay off da radar blood."

"Iight OG. We got you." I lied turning around with a demon grin. If that nigga only knew. We filled the demons up with go'sin preparation to set the streets on fire. After we damn near brought the convenience store out, we were out." I got them bands for who eva make it back to da word first. If I win, yall niggas owe me a band a piece." I slammed my door and took off for a cheating head start. Pilling the rubber of the tiers marking the pavement. I left them niggas in smoke."

I hopped back on 64 going back West. Not to my surprise, Wolf was coming up in my rearview fast. Behind him was Qua, his car was accompanied by Jowan and Jo-Jo. Even though I had it, you know damn well my greedy ass won't try to give up ten bands to none of these niggas. Wolf and Qua rode lane to lane going neck to neck for a second-place ticket. Even though there was no prize for second place. Deep in last place was one of my niggas named B. He was black as hell and so young, bald head as a motherfucker. So to sum it all up, we just called him B. He was weaving through the traffic with terrifying speed. I'm talking about the type of speed that almost move me to want to pull over and get the fuck out the nigga way my damn self.

I accepted the Challenge and turned up the intro to Lil Baby's Harder Than Ever. After turning the music up, I turned the speed up to match the paste of the rapper's flow. Through the rearview, I could see the distance growing between my competitive peers and me. B was no longer in last place by this time, taking his right for a place in fourth. Quickly, he was closing in on both Wolf and Qua. I laughed my ass off when I noticed Juwana and Jo Jo crazy asses hanging out the windows of the car teasing Wolf as Qua fought hard to take the second-place lead.

Then, hold up. That's why B was hauling ass the way he was. It was black and white with flashing lights on his trail. That nigga won't race for the paper. He was racing for freedom. I turned down the sounds of the music and flipped open the burner phone.

"Hello" She answered on the first ring.

"Ayeee, yeah Lil Shawty we're on 64 West. Five SRT Demons in different colors in a high-speed chase. So far, I only…"

"Ight, I had already caught a call to go back up. How I had a feeling it was you? Again! I thought we talked about moving a little smarter?"

"Look not right now please. Get on with your job and preach later."

"Well, there's two cars that already responded to da call. If yall can get rid of dem three, we can catch da rest and stall dem. Also, I'll see if we can misdirect da third car, right…'Bout…Now" As she said, the car was flying down the ramp pulling up right next to my car. I grabbed the gun in my lap and thought about sending a few shots at the pig. Then I said fuck it and decided to put my trust in my driving skills. At least I was confident that I had a great plan B.

I slightly swerved right trying to scare the police car off the road. The driver flinched causing the car to jerk but quickly got this shit together. Actually, the fucker grew some balls and tried to run his car back into mine. Wasn't good enough buddy. Wisely, I just simply changed over to the next lane. That threw his whole measurement off. While embracing for impact, all he caught was an open lane. He lost control of the wheel causing the car to fishtail way left. Damn near cutting off the path for Qua and wolf.

Qua quickly swerved right, spinning his wheel immediately back left to go around the black and white that was starting to spin out of control. Wolf, having a focused eye on the road, saw the accident waiting to happen long before it did, and was already picking up more speed. He zoomed past the rotating car only catching a minor impact on his bumper from the front end of the police car. After that, it was over with copper. The next thing I knew, the car was crashing into the wall that ran through the middle of the highway. That was easy. What they don't have is driving school in the academy. I guess practice is nothing like having real experience. "One down," I said, talking to the phone lying in my lap next to the gun.

"Boy, what did you do?" Lil Shawty asked through the speakerphone.

"Shidd. None." You know, it's been a long time since I've actually told the truth. I really didn't do anything this time. Just changed lanes. Now we had another problem which was the initial issue. B was now caught up with Wolf and Qua. So was the police crusher that attempted to chase us down. This one was an aggressive little fucker too. He sped straight past the fifth car sitting in last place and went directly for B. He rammed his car into the back end of B's car with no remorse. B picked up speed trying to outdrive the black and white that was tightly pressed on his bumper. B drove up in between Wolf and Qua's now giving both of them on each side of his whip. Wisely, they both slowed their speed in an attempt to close in on the police car. I wished I was back there to have that bitch in my trap. I would've jumped to plan B and taken his head off his shoulders, stopping him right in his tracks.

The police car steered right slamming into Qua's car pretty hard. So hard that his car fell all the way over to the shoulder of the road. For a minute, I thought it was over for them. Luckily though, they only came within inches. Qua put the tires back on the road and got back into position. With vengeance, Qua called his car up against the side of the police car, the black and white jerked left due to lack of control. Wolf slammed the black and white back to the right side of its lane. That caused the car to have another impact on Qua's car. One of the tires on the back of the police car

popped loose. Qua rode to avoid the lost tire flying over to his lane. Instead, his back tire rolled over the top of it and his car was lifted to two wheels. Before it was too late, he went to apply all four tires back on the road. From the force of speed and motivation, the car was lifted to its other two wheels on the opposite side. Losing balance, the car flipped over multiple times. While doing so, the police car was uncontrollably driving off the road, through the side rail, and over the cliff of the highway. By the time Qua's car was flipping, it landed on its hood. "Umm/Dats two down. But we need an ambulance to pull up like right now. It's a white SRT with three juveniles. I need you to make sure dey are well and get dem to da hospital ASAP please."

"Making da call now."

"Ayee"

"Yes"

"If there is any questions which I know 'der will be, just say dat it was a loose tire on the highway dat caused dem to crash."

"Got you. Gotta go. Yall get da fuck out dem cars."

Chapter 52
Q'S Quest of Queen

Scene: In traffic

"Damn cuz, dem nigga sputtin' on fo' da R out dis bitch." Dat was Top Shoota riding shotgun in the Rolls Royce. He was referring to a handful of SRTs that were speeding past the highway exceedingly.

"Dem niggas gone get somebody killed" I was already decelerating the needle on my miles per hour meter. I wasn't trying to be anywhere near them when that shit happened. In fact, I'm getting off at the next exit.

"Aye cuz, I finally got dat data you asked me to search for too." I got anxious and excited at the news Top Shotta had just revealed. He owed a big favor to me. Little known to me, I had served an obligant to him last summer. We were reunited on the beach of Virginia. Some time after that, my old-time friend landed right in my backyard Uterary. He was trying to lie low from some troubles in the Tidewater area. I gave him and his people a few places to settle until he was ready to regroup and head back.

"Oh yeah, I knew you would come through for a nigga. Wat you get?' I got off the highway using the mechanics' live exit next to Whitcomb Court Projects.

I had to cut Top Shotta off before he got too far ahead "Nigga! We can do whatever da fuck we wanna do. Just don't get caught.'

"You can't hide from da all-seeing eye Q" Top Shotta was looking over at me with some type of disparaged unsettled expression.

"Did I say all dat when you needed me? Was I trying to give you a speech in yo' desperate time of need? You think I don't know wat da fuck we're into? Wat, you'd don't trust me? You don't think I got you like you got me?"

"Naw, cuz I know how we rock. I just want you to make sure dat you open dat door."

Top Shotta, dat info, please? Fo' I drop yo' ass off in da middle of Mosby and leave you der." Top Shotta started laughing but I flashed a look of grave meaning.

"Come on cuz. You ok? I'ma G. I can swing through any jungle. Da fuck you thought." He handled a man's piece of paper. It's an address. You ain't get da shit from me through." I cut an eye at the niggas as to say spit it out already. "Soon Q, do order is going to call on you to make a major sacrifice.' I looked confused. Damn near dumbfounded.

"Wat do you mean? Supreme said dat I wouldn't have to do no shit like dat."

'Yeah, my nigga. Dat was before."

"Before what?" I was growing highly agitated and impatient on top of that, I was getting there fast.

"Before Q Jr."

I slammed on the brakes causing the tires of the car to stop in the middle of the Martin Luther King Jr's bridge. "So you tell me now? Let's not forget to stick to the story. I'm not trying to be set up as an illustration. But basically, yeah. Either or."

"Him or me huh? Same ol'story.' I slammed my hands back on the steering wheel before pulling off, getting back into traffic.

"Yeah cauz. I wish I could tell you dat I knew a way out of dis fo you. But I only know of one way."

"I think I know a way."

"Oh yeah. Wat do you know dat I don't?"

"Kill Supreme" Top Shotta said nothing. In fact, my last suggestion had silenced him for the rest of the ride. I pulled up to his drop-off destination and addressed him before he stepped out.

"Listen Top Shotta, I know you got your own life to live and shit to live up to. I'm not going to ask you to fall into dis trap wit me. I'ma do wat I need to do in order to handle my business on my own. All I need you to do is keep quiet. You know wat dey would do to me if words get out dat I even thought about some crazy things like dis. But….Top Shotta was already pushing the door open preparing to make his exit. On his way out, he held one of his index fingers up to his lips. He was right. As he made his leave, so did I.

My next stop was at the address written on the paper. Pulling up to the location, I found that it was just as Ms. Buffy said, A gated community off Old Brook Road. The gate was fenced around nice and beautiful full-size houses. They had garages attached to them. Some two, many one. Although I had a good vibe at my distance, I still had the slightest idea as to how I would open the gate to allow me access into the community.

I was sitting at the top of the gate for a good little while now, trying to figure out a way to get in and an idea had swept through my mind. A Nissan 300ZX Anniversary '93 with the T-Top was slowly approaching the gate. The driver scanned a key card and the gates were unrestricted. Switching the gear into drive, I slightly pulled away from the curb and tried my best to blend in with the small car traveling in front of me.

Mission accomplished. Now though, I knew that it was only the first trailer test. Subsequently, a tall booth was up ahead. The old-school 300Z was able to roll right on past it going over the speed bump. A level was dropped down in front of my car. A window to the tell house had quickly slid open."Umm. Excuse me sir?" She asked me through my window as soon as I was able to drop it." Who are you? I ain't never seen your car 'round here. And you are not on da registry or da guest list. So...Where do you think you're going? You do know dat dis is a private property and dat wat you are doing is called trespassing right?" She was a skinny white young lady. Pretty tanned skin. Hair wrapped up in c.bun. The most notable thing to me about the woman was her personality. How she talked with a loud ascent from up North mixed with Southern Slang. If my eyes were closed, I would have sworn that I was talking to a...You know what? Never mind. Something else stood out to me about the woman. It was a ring. I had a dear understanding of the log on the ring. I should open my eyes more often to things like this. They were...Well, I guess I could say we were everywhere.

"I'm traveling from da east, making my way back home." Was wat I felt the need to say now that I knew what she stood for.

"Uh huh?" She looked distorted as if I was trying to hoodwink her. "Wat did you say?' That was the wrong response. With one more era, I had the right to violate her. I gave her a sign of a thousand words demonstrating how I would annihilate her if I found out that she was faking the way of life." Oh umm. I'm so sorry sir. Who are you traveling wit?" That's a good girl. Still thinking, I stared a hole in her head and could see that she was extremely frightened.

"Wit da one who gives guidance." There was nothing more for me to say. I opened my window and waited for the level to be lifted. After waiting only a split second on what was expected to happen, I continued on with my advancement.

I parked a few yards away from the mailbox sitting on the curb. I had to look down at the marked piece of paper to make sure that the address was identical. Seeing that they were, I scanned my brain for a logical explanation as to why the hell was this corny-ass Nissan Z 300 Anniversary parked in the driveway. I slid the gear into the park and decided to sit and wait for the answer to my question like I've done so many times before.

Climbing out of the Nissan Z 300 was a dark skin man standing at about my height. With the same similar skinny frame that I used to have. He had a short dreaded high-top fade, something of the likes of Bob Simpson. Had a pair of casual dress shoes and slacks. Topped off with a plaid button-up shirt. Carrying a handful of dozen roses. This dorky Steve Urkel, minus the glasses, looking motherfucker made his way up to the doorstep. Alright, maybe I was just hating a little bit. I guess you could say the dude had some type of class. He rang the doorbell which was a good sign. At least he didn't have a key.

The front door opened and there she was. Just as beautiful as I remember. She wore her nursing uniform which was an upgraded version from the last time I saw her. It seemed as if she had gained some weight over these past months. I hope it wasn't due to pregnancy. She greeted the man I knew as a stranger with a heartbreaking smile and a warm welcoming hug. She even did that thing I loved so much when she lifted her right leg while enjoying his hug. I knew because she used to do the same thing with me. That was a while back. I guess times have changed now and that I was easily replaceable.

Keyshia still looked the same physically. It was hard for me to tell how she felt, though. If I had the right to assume, I would say that she looked pretty happy to me. She grabbed the flowers that the home-wrecking geek bought for her. You know that temptation song where they said "I wish it would rain?" That's how I feel right now. I wished it would rain down on their happiness. Then again, maybe not because that might force them inside.

For now, they stood on the porch discussing words that were out of my range. After all that I've been through trying to get back to this woman and she couldn't even wait.

Alright, look, I know, so don't play me like I'm stupid, selfish, or spiteful! She doesn't know. But does that mean that she should pick up and move on that fast? Even if I really was dead. I'll let you be the judge of that. Before you do, just know that I'm not talking about the house. I'm talking about the heart. Shouldn't I still have a seat at the bottom of her heart? Guess I haven't conquered all the bottoms I've touched. If I would have known that she had given up so fast, then maybe I would have done the same. I would have gone after Flex if I knew that this moment would be this.

Underneath all of those ill feelings, I still loved her. I could lie to you all day and not give two fuckers whether you beloved me or not. One thing I knew for certain was that there was no way in this lie or the next that I could lie to myself. I love Keyshia so much that it was agape, platonic. In layman's terms. I was willing to suffer just to see her happy. Throughout this whole process, the beat of my heart was the only thing that kept me trying. Now, even that part of me had experienced a symbolic form of death. Closing the casket to my heart, they sealed my suspicion with a kiss.

Shifting the car into drive, I made a U-turn on the widened street and made my way out of their business. Seems like I was running again huh? Felt like I had to before I ended up killing somebody. I'd have to find another way to run into my daughters. They still had another good hour before they got out of school. I pulled up early thinking that I was gone fuck some pussy up before they got there. But I guess a nigga beat me to that punch.

Chapter 53
Keyshai's 1st Kiss Goodbye

Scene: Her Home

Another long day of work. After another long night of loneliness from the lack of love, my life has been filled with the most expensive misery I've ever known to exist. There was no luck in me finding Q's body at all. Even though my suspicions were still riding high, I had no one to help me. It seemed as if no one even cared. Made a bitch feel crazy and delusional. Maybe I was, maybe my life was just a made-up twist of tales in someone's sick wicked schemes. Thank God there was a ringing of the doorbell sounding throughout my house. I never had company over. Although there was this one.

Looking through the peephole. I knew it couldn't be anyone else but him. I opened the door with a half smile. Just trying not to seem so rude. "Hey Derck!" I was just happy to see anybody. I swear I was not trying to lead him in the wrong way. "You brought flowers again Derek was a neighbor of mine from a few feet down. He approached me one day as we both checked our mailboxes in a synchronizing order. Ever since that day, he would try his best to talk me into being his. He was smart, nice, and kind of huh…Different. The only issue I had was that my heart was still so strongly stuck to Q's; I was in absolutely no condition to be in a relationship with anyone else unless it was Q.

"Hey beauty. How has your day been?" Derek said that beauty was my name for him. I liked it. Thought it fit perfectly. So I let him slide.

"It's been ok I guess I could say. A lil better now dat I have des beautiful flowers." I removed the roses from his hands and cradled them in my arms with a respectful smile.

'I would do anything just to brighten up your day. You are so worthy of real love. Something that I am certain I can provide you with. All you have to do is open your heart and give me a chance, Keyshia. All I'm asking is for a chance." Sounds like he was begging me. Nigga, ain't even get a piece of the pussy. Don't even know what it smells like. I've grown into a decent woman. In my latter days, I was known to be a savage. I didn't want some pushover as a man. Besides, my heart was open. It was torn in half; wide the fuck open. Derek was a good guy to whom I was open.

"Listen Derek, I appreciate it. I really do. But I'm just not in a mental state to focus on a relationship. With my career taking off and I have my daughters to take care of. I just don't think dat now is da right time. I would not forgive myself for doing something as selfish as asking or making you wait. Hope you understand?"

'Na, I don't understand. I can provide for you and your daughters. Everything you need and more. What is it? You're not attracted to me because I'm not a thug?" I laughed in my head, which was good; I barely had a chance to do that nowadays." Then when a brother runs off with a white girl, sisters want to look at a brother like he" Oh my God, boy shut up! See I'm glad you were here to see for yourself. A bitch ain't got time for all that sympathy shit. I let Derek continue to cry himself to a river while my eyes roamed my environment. They landed on the shining Pearl Rolls Royce parked a little ways from my house. I've never seen that car behind these gates before, unless the neighbors had a new car or some super-rich company. I didn't know who the car belonged to. For some strange reason though, I was pulled to the car. Attracted to it. I wanted so badly to walk right up to the car and take a seat inside. Not just because of the luxury of the car, or its estimated price. But just because it felt as if I deserved to. As if I belong there. Something I couldn't explain at all.

"Keyshia look, I just wanted to come by and remind you just in case you forgot, that tomorrow, I will be heading down south to Miami. This is our last chance. You could pack up and leave with me"

"No Derek. Like I told you before, I have my own life here. I barely know you. And my kids don't know you at all and I'm fine wit dat. All of it."

"Ok well, can I at least get a goodbye kiss maybe it would change your mind a little?"

"Umm..." I wanted to decline so badly. But he was so nice. Besides, what would a little kiss hurt?"Ok, I guess." He leaned in for the kiss, taking aim at my lips. Having second thoughts already, I slightly turned my head and offered him my left cheek instead. I looked over and noticed the Rolls Royce was pulling off. Which meant that someone was in the car behind the dark tints the entire time. Was somebody watching me? Who would do some creepy shit like that? Moments after, Derek was pulling his car out of my driveway. I was just as happy when he left as I was when he came.

Chapter54
For Swearing Flex

Scene: St. John Street

"Ight, ight. I hear you. Yeah, I ight don't make me choke da shit out yo ass next time. I see you. Ight, look, I gotta go. "That was Lil Shawty, I got bad news. What's new right? None of the youngins in the car crash made it out alive. Qua had a chance but lost the fight on his way to the hospital. We parked the four cars that did make it back on each side of St. John street. I slid the phone into my pocket, grabbed the pistol, tucked that, and hopped out of my all-green demon. Even though I was out of the Demon, I still had a demon inside of me. "Yall niggas owe me a band a piece," was the first thing I made clear.

"Maine fuck dat' B said in jitters" Did yall see what happened to Qua's and dem whip?"

"Yeah," Blu answered, standing beside the red SRT. Dat ma'fucka flipped like 45 times. I almost ran into dat bitch."

"Yall think dem lil niggas ight?" Wolf questioned.

"Dey ain't make it" I simply answered as if everything was fine while slamming my car door. All them nigga was now looking at me like."

"How da fuck did you know dat?" yeah, like what B just said. But you know what? That was a good question. How else would I know other than the only way I knew?

"I just know B" I avoided the question but really made no attempt to provide the means of my information. "Da whole fuckin car just flipped some shit of times after going ova 100 mph. Dis ait'n no fuckign movie. If dey make it out of dat, dey ass got an army of angels with dem."

"No bullshit," Blu agreed." Da ma fucka was rolling like a dice in a game of Cee-lo. Niggas ready be hurt 'bout dis one. We gotta go break da news to da gang."

Chapter 55
Quick Wanted Q

"Umm…..Q. Are you ok?" Dawn asked, walking up behind the couch massaging my shoulders. I didn't reply. Really didn't feel like talking." I noticed you've been kind off out of it fo' da ass few days. Is there some on yo' mind dat you need to talk 'bout?"

"Naw, I'm good right now.' I tried to put some warmth in my words to the coldness of my heart.

"Are you sure? You seem very teased right now. If there's a problem, you know' you can let me know."And don't fo'get the fact dat we made a pack of no to lie to each other."

"Naw, never dat. I just need some time to think. Put some shit into its proper plans."

"Well, while you do dat, can I use da car to go pick up a couple of things please?"

"Go ahead. I'on care. Shiddd, take your time."

"Thank you. Jr. is in deep sleep. He should be out for a while and I'll be right back. Talking about taking my time, I heard dat ugly. You know' I can't stay away from you fo' too long. Love you." She ain't even wait for me to say I loved her back, which I think I did but was unsure because I didn't even know if I had the heart to love with.

I think that was way past the time for me to hop back into the streets. Looking back on my past wishes, I had received everything that I wanted. One of those biggest things was time. Time to plan my return. I was back. All I needed was a plan. When you start your process of planning, you have to have an objective in mind. Once that was established, you should see your plan from the end first then the beginning. Now plan your first step. By the time it was all said and done, I wanted to make sure that my son was safe and protected and then get my revenge on Flex. Before I took the air out of his lungs though. I would first take everything he had away from him. Everything he worked for. Everything he stole and took, and left him without anything, he deserved nothing. I'll show that nigga exactly how it felt to have everything you wanted snatched away from you. Then I would leave his dirty ass hanging out to dry like some clean clothes on the line.

I felt no need in announcing my markup in finical value because I ain't really give a fuck about money anymore. But for those who do care, I was well over the million dollars mark. As long as I knew my daughters were straight and I made sure that my son was ok. I ain't give a fuck about anybody else. All of my peers that I grew up with were dying and didn't get to see them go. Couldn't even say goodbye. 99% of the ones that remained didn't give a fuck. Why should I? Fuck, I looked like trying to save a world full of people who weren't open and willing to give two fucks? Don't answer that. Not important. Right now, I'm just rambling. Feel free to judge me. Fuck it. You have seen or heard about the shit that I've been through. Better yet, how about this, you put yourself in my shoes and then judge yourself. That way, we won't have any reason to dispute the disagreements.

Fuck all that though. Do me a small favor and go kick rocks somewhere, then double back to holler at me. I'm about to cook up a plan. Show these niggas they don't fucked with the wrong one.

Chapter 56
Dawn Divulged

Scene: Her crib

"It's already been a little over an hour since I've been away from Q and the baby. I hadn't planned to be out for this long. Q has been giving off some very strong vibes of unstableness lately. Ever since I've known him, that has always been one of his strong suits. His frequency has been signaling a lot of static for weeks now. He's always been cool, calm, and collected. But even with those same traits today, I could tell that he wasn't fully in control of his thoughts. If your thoughts were out of toot, then that could definitely affect your actions. Even Q taught me that. Like I said, he's done a good job until this point. I've had this very same feeling before. Back in, he slipped out of my sight and thought that I had lost him forever. Not again. I had to hurry up and get back to him.

This was my last stop which was a dreaded one. I had to come here to pick up a few things from my apartment. For the life of me, I couldn't understand why Q insisted that I hold onto this rudery piece of shit. Trying to put a finger on it, I assumed that this was a part of him that he was missing. Like he was homesick. I don't know why? That nigga must have been really crazy underneath that shell of his. If he considered choosing this over what we had. I don't know many of them too well, but one thing that this whole city knows about the Jackson ward niggas was that they had ward pride and were built ward tough.

It looked different out here today though. Maybe it was because I haven't been out here in such a long time. Maybe it was the spring season sun shining down on the smiles that made this life seem so harmless. So, alright. Like everything was ok. Couldn't fool a bitch like me though. I've seen this shit before. It was a repeating cycle that happened over and over, and over again. Like watching close drying in the dryer. Even when I had to lay my head here, I always tried my best to go unseen. The frame of my body never allowed that to go as planned. Now, it was the body of the car that had everyone looking even though I knew they couldn't see through the tints. I knew also that they would not take their eyes off this car until they figured out who operated it. Or until it rolled out of their sight. Luckily for them, I had just left the hair salon. I was willing to try out my new look on the spectators.

Parking the car on St. John, I made my way to my apartment. As I traveled through with a dynamite presence destined to pop, I fell in love with the reactions in the hood. Most of these bitches always hate their little hearts. That was always a good song. This means that I was most definitely doing something right. I was so cute. Like the cherry on top of a sundae. I did have to give credit to the few girls who admired real elegance when they saw it. There wasn't a nigga out here blessed with eyes to see that wasn't on me. Many had the balls to try their hand at the game they played. And then cursed me out with the same tongue when I ignored them. I was here for one purpose in mind. Other than that, I was itching to get back to my man. Yall heard that? I got a man bitches. I hope he was in the mood to scratch this kitty.

In and out just as I planned. Small bag in hand, I made my way back to the car. It's like my exit was waiting on me. The number of people in front had grown. The sidewalks were closed and packed so much so that I damn near had to squeeze my way through. All I know is that I better not get touched by a soul. If so, I'm reaching in this bag and whipping this baby Glock 40. Q brought it for me. It was pink and black; I loved the color coordination. I also knew to use this bitch now. He even took me to the shooting range on many occasions to upgrade my experience. It gave me a taste of power. I urged to test my skills out on a motherfucker. Like this nigga for example.

Flex had some nerve to be leaning up against my baby daddy's car. Maybe he thought it was mine. Either way, he was dead wrong. Q was so successful since his return that he even helped me succeed in such a short time. I knew that it had to be hate that kept him from reaching out to his own blood brother and getting him a helping hand. I was starting to even think that Flex tried to kill Q, and he knew it was him. I wouldn't be surprised; It fits Flex perfectly. Maybe that explains why Q laid so low, or kept himself wrapped in his works and studies. Or maybe he was doing what he does best, planning.

"Excuse me boy, who gave you permission?' I snapped with a sense, attitude using my hand to make a gesture to Flex to get the fuck up.

"Oh cuss me miss. My bad. Damn, Dis you right here?" Here we go with this weak as games gain. I thought, rolling my eyes to the back of my head "You know?" Flex asked, starting to stand up straight.

"No," I replied. "I don't want to know."

"Fo about a half a year, I've been trying to figure out exactly who dis car belonged to." He made sure I knew anyway" I knew it was somebody special behind the wheel of all exclusive machine." No, that was lame too." But now dat I know it's you, I stand corrected.' Huh? I only said in my head but the frown on my face was clearly a replacement for the word confusion. "You don't know how disappointed I am to find out it's just you. Wat da fuck are you doing wit a car like dis? Where do you get da money from? Like what's really new Shawty? You think you better than us bums out here? Den you got da nerve to pull up stuntin' on ma'fukas. Who da fuck do you think you are bitch? Matter fact, I'on even give a fuck who you thought up was, I'ma show you exactly who you are. Don't allow anything to happen out here without going through me. Now get da fuck on fo I car jack up fake boogie ass bitch!"

Ok, now I am growing a little nervous. I could see the devil's horns growing out of this niggas head as his face turned red from the steam heating up his body temperature. I did what he said I should. Even though Flex just talked to me like I was a stepped-on piece of shit, he had the right one today though. I'ma make sure I showed him exactly who the fuck I knew I was. The bitch of a ghost!

Chapter 57
Q Dives In
Scene: His spot

Right now, my hands held the only thing that fully made me happy these days. Not even Dawn could fill this void. "Brah you goofy as hell." Jr. Looked into my eyes while giggling in my face. I leaned in to blow air against his bare tummy making farting sounds. That shit tickled little dude all the way to his funny bone. It doesn't take much to make him smile. He barely cried. But this little game of ours always made him droll in laughter.

Finally, Dawn was walking through the door. I heard her make an entrance, but Baby Q spotted her first. At the sight of her, his face immediately started to glow with more glee. Bouncing, kicking his legs and swinging his arms in excitement. Dawn was a great mother. Jr knew it and had every reason to love her the way everybody should love their mother. "You see mommy. You see dat lady?" In between questions, I blew on his belly again. "She is coming to get you. Here, she's coming." Baby voice.

"Well, look at all having all da fun and stuff." Dawn came over and took a seat next to us on the couch. "Come to mommy baby." She talked to Jr. while taking him off my hands.

"Ok, I see you got dat weave done," I joked to Dawn. "Wat, you went to New York or some other place to make dat happen? She playfully pushed me on my shoulder.

No, I had to make a few more stops. What do you think though? Do you like it?"

"Yeah, it's different. It definitely fits you and it brings out your cute lil ears."

"Q stop playing. You for real?"

"Hell yeah, I'm for real; I like up lil ears. Plus I don't spend all dat money on earrings just so you can hide dem wit yo' hair." "
Well, thank you for everything." She leaned in to lay a thick kiss on my lips.

"Umm, what, are you trying to get it in or something? Cause we can put Jr in da swing right quick. Shiddd…I ain't gotta be long."

Dawn laughed a happy laugh before her face turned serious. "No babe, not right now. But I do need to talk to you."

"You're talking to me now." I was still joking.

"Q for real."

"Ight now fo' real. Wat' sup?" I asked matching her energy.

"Well being dat you are in such a good mode right now, I really don't want to tell you dis. It's really been a while since I've seen you like dis and I would hate to be da cause to deflate dat smile."

"Ok. Well, don't do it, den." I simply suggested. "If it's something that's gone piss me off. I ain't tryna hear dat shit right now anyway."

"I understand dat baby. But you are always preaching bout honesty and how we should absolutely not leave each other in da dark about things. Well dis is urgent and definitely important for you to know". I was just looking at her waiting for her to say whatever it was that she was trying to say. "I just left from 'round Jackson Ward. "ok…Get on with it already. I hoped she left the why out because I really didn't care. "Anddd….I ….ran in-to…Flex". "Now she has my undivided attention.

"Ok." I urged her to continue.

"So, I came out from my apartment and he leaned up against da car. I asked him to move. Maybe not in da most polite way, but I wasn't disrespectful. Anyway, dis nigga talked to me as if I was a dog. Literarily, all in me and all types of bitches and some more. He threatened to carjack me and said he would do something to me if he saw me out der in dat car again.'

He threatens you?" She nodded her head. "Did he follow you here?" She shook her head. "Are you sure Dawn?"

"Yes Q. I was scared out of my mind. Of course, I made sure I wasn't being followed,"

"Ok. Keep going."

"He said dat he has been eyeing da car fo' sometime now and dat he was trying to figure out who da car belongs to. I guess he was mad 'cause he thinks da a car belongs to me."

"Now, dat ain't why he is mad. He is mad because he can't have you. And he is thinking you are getting money and he ain't eating off your plate.

He tried to blame me in front of da whole Projects, saying dat I think I'm better than the rest of dem out over. Dat I was tryna shot on dem. Q, I don't even know dem people like dat. I'm not like dat. You know' dat."

"Look, fuck Flex and any of dem mafukca's who feel some type of way about you. Did dat nigga put his hands on you at all? Even a fingernail?"

'Naw, if his ass would have, I would have shot his ass."

"Good thing you didn't have to do dat." By now I would be sitting up on the couch reaching for my shoes. "Dat nigga crazy. You would have definitely had to kill him. Or he would have..."I shook my head.

"Anyway, I don't want dat on your hands." Both shoes on, laces tide, I stood tall.

"Q, wat are you bout to do?" I could see the sudden stress on her face.. "Please don't do none stupid. We need you. I looked from her to my son.

"When do I ever do some stupid? Da last stupid thing I did was trust dat snake. I tucked both of my pistols and was now considered fully dressed. "Look, I'll be back. Don't wait on me and don't fucin' leave." I headed to the door.

"Dequan!" Dawn called for me like somebody was trying to kill her ass. I turned around with a questioning look on my face."Can I get a kiss before you leave Please?" I'll give her that. I walked over to tongue her down. She kissed as if she expected this to be our last one or something. I won't be going out like that this time baby girl. I could almost promise that. "Don't you need da car keys?"

"Naw, I'm good. I'll see y'all later." Off the elevator, I stopped at the desk in the lobby. "Can you make sure dat no one goes up to my place and dat my son and his mother are safe and sound?"

"Sure," The receptionist assured. "Is everything ok? Is there anything else I could help you with?"

"Uh…Yeah. Matter fact, there is. Do we have any extra cars to drive round here?"

"Not a problem sir." The receptionist reached under the counter and came back holding a tray full of car keys in her hands. She laid the tray on the table allowing me to choose my preference. They were all luxury cars. Too stand outish.

"Umm…Anything a little less…"

"Ooh. I understand." Some motion different try with a new set of keys. These were more like it. I picked up the keys to a Yukon Denali. "Umm, it's the second garage down.

Keypad code 12366."

Scene 2: Jackson Ward

In no time, I was pulling up the hill of St. James Street. I hopped out of the truck and made my way to the targeted door. It was locked but after a few knocks, the door was being opened.

"Q! Wat da fuck?" It was Stan. He was magnifying in his greeting as he should be. Shit, everybody thought I was still dead. This was step one to my plan. Make them believe little by little. Stan still rocked the iced-out diamond and gold angle that I had given him last year. That makes me smile.

"Ayee come brah. I need you to ride with me." I was already heading back to the car climbing into the back seat.

Stan followed all the while asking one of the questions. "Wat da hell are we 'bout to do? Where da fuck did you come from brah? I hope you ain't ready to take me on no dummy mission?"

"Stan!" I had to settle him down. "Drive da car." He turned around in front of the passenger seat and looked at me laid down in the back seat of the truck.

"Aww lord. Don't tell me you still on dat incognito, fake ghost shit brah? Dat's why you are shit in da first place. Now you're trying to get me in some shit. Where are we going fool?"

"Go get Reggie. Tell him to get in da car. DO NOT tell anybody I'm in here."

"Ain't nobody looking fo' yo' ass Q." Stan was pushing the truck up the hill. "Everybody thinks' sneaky ass' is dead. In case you fo'got." I could tell where we were from my position by the top of the project buildings. Stan slowed the vehicle as he rolled down Saint John Street. A Lot of people noticed it was him and tried to flag him down, which was good. It killed the suspicion that may arise from an intruder. "There goes Reggie right there on da Brickyard front," Stan announced.

"Good. Hit dat horn. Tell his ass to come over here and get him in da car. "While giving instructions to Stan, I was pulling one of my pistols from under my designer belt. Stan caught a glimpse of that.

"Hope you ain't just use me to do no snake shit a?"

"Man, jus' get da nigga in da car." Now, I was climbing back into the third row of seats.

"Ayee wat's up Shawty?" Reggie said while he approached the truck. "I see you came outside to play today?"

"Get in nigga. Roll wit me."Stan offered.

"Wat dis a new whip? Or dis is just another one of yo' bitches joining?"

"Now, do a loaner." Stan was pulling off back into the street.

"Wats up through nigga? Where da hell are we going?" Reggie asked.

"Up," was all I said after creeping back up to the second row of seats. Gun resting in my lap. Finger on the trigger. Reggie looked back and for the first time in my life, I spotted fear in his eyes. Even if it were only for a split second for a good half of a minute though, he was silenced.

"Mainee...Wat da fuck!?" Reggie's eyes were wide open as if he was being electrocuted.

"Dats da same shit I said," Stan said.

"Q, where da fuck have you been? How da fuck are you here?"

"I said dat too," Stan said.

Is dis nigga fo' real? Like in real life?" Reggie looked over to Tan while panting back at me. "Wats up wit da tool though?" Reggie looked back towards me, "What yall niggas trying to bring me a move? If you are looking fo' da nigga dat tried to kill you brah, I am too. I ain't do it. I can't even find da nigga my damn self."

"Now don't trip big brah." I spoke. "I know who tried to kill me. I only got dis tool because I know' yo' as retarded. I wasn't sure how you would handle seeing a ghost."

"Oh my God" Reggie said, smacking his forehead. "You still on dis ghost shit? Well, at least you definitely know how to play your role.

"I said da same shit brah," Stand said while nodding his head in agreement.

"Who tried to kill you though brah. Let's go take dat nigga's head off right now!" Reggie was getting hyped as he switched into his killer mode. "It was dat snake ass nigga Flex, won't it? I already knew it. I jus' ain't have no proof. How da fuck yo own brother try to kill you?" I won't even say anything, Reggie was basically talking to himself.

"I'ma handle dat," I said putting my gun up."We need to pick everybody else up. Big Dee, Hawk, and Burga" Stan and Reggie both got quiet. I ain't think nothing of it. I'd rather have it like this.

"Burga gone bruh," was all Reggie said.

"Wat do you mean to be gone? Where did he go? We can go get him." Stan and Reggie looked at each other.

"He went to da grave. He is gone." Now I was silenced.

"How da fuck did he die?"

"He got shot in da head by one of his own guns," he said.

"Who da fuck shot him?"

"Flex"

"Wat!?"Who the fuck do this nigga think he is? As a matter of fact, who the fuck was this nigga? He had to be processed by the devil himself. This is the brother I thought I knew from childhood.

"It was an accident," Stan cleared up. "If you gone tell it, say it right." Right maybe I'm trying to kill myself was an accident too, huh?

"Go get da other two."I was done talking.

"You know Big Dee da bottom. I think Hawk by Tiger mart." Gave the drops to Stan.

Moments later, I was back resting in the third row of the seat with Big Dee and Hawk seated in the row in front of me.

"You know," I said, sitting up in the back seat.' Yall niggas should really do a better job at being aware of yall surrounding."

Big Dee and Hawk looked back startled. Damn near jumping out of their bodies at the sight of me. "Wat da fuck?" They shouted in harmony.

"Dat's da same shit we said." Stan and Reggie said unified.

"Ayeee Q, I should shoot yo' ass in da face fo' popping up on niggas like dat. Wat type of shit you on nigga?" Big Dee laughed at Hawk's statement. I shook my head knowing that I could have had him dead only a few seconds ago. That's not what I was here for though.

"Ight, jus' listen. I need yall niggas to spare me some time right quick. So I'ma make dis fast. I'm pretty sure everybody would have da same thing to say about me being alive, so we skipped dat part please. Also, I think it would be a wise decision dat we keep dis between us only. Tomorrow is Wednesday, garbage dat. Reggie, Big Dee, and Hawk, yall niggas need to be at da curb at East Federall and 2nd Street at 5:30 a.m. sharp. Do not be late. After my people dumb the cause, they gone be replaced with bags. Y'all get'em and break 'em down between each other. It's enough fo' all yall. No need for any of dat greedy shit. Dat way, yall can cut dat nigga Flex completely off. He thinks yall need him, now, I'm given yall the power to cut his water off."

"Where da fuck you been all dis time?' Hawked asked, frustrated.

"Not right now Hawk," I replied.

"Naw, for real though brah. Don't tell me you were out here da whole time and left niggas to suffer in da hands of dat petty ass brother of yours when you could have been helpin'? You could have popped out and took shit over. know' we got yo' back."

"No bullshit," Big Dee agreed.

"It's all 'bout time." Pace and execution. "I schooled them. "Plus dis ain't about me. I'm doing dis shit for yall. So yall can spread yall wings."

"Wat bout you?" Big Dee asked. "You gone be over when we need da re-up right?"

"Naw bruh, I'm out dis shit. I go other shit popping. Ain't no love out here anyway."   "Shidd...I love you nigga!" Reggie exclaimed.

"Me too nigga."Said Stan.

"No bullshit brah. Tighten up wit dat soft shit," said Big Dee. I cut my eyes over at Hawk. "Wat?'He asked. "Don't look at me. I mean I fuck wit you and all dat 'bout"

"Now though yall." I cut Hawk off. "I'm straight. Fo' me to put myself in da game again would be selfish, stupid and just in da way. Yall nigga eat and find yo way. I at least owe dis much to da gang. I'm a plug yall into da socket though."

"Wat bout me though fool?' Stan asked

"You know I got you big brah. Don't trip."

Chapter 58
Reggie Touchdown to Cause Hell

Scene: E Federal and 2nd Street

"Da garbage truck coming down now fool." Big Dee stated. I looked up to catch it coming around the corner. It was perfect timing. Yesterday he left us to handle whatever that was so important, you know how that nigga be, he left us a key to an apartment; on the very same corner that we stood on. Don't ask me how he got the shit done. It's like I just met the nigga for the first time.

"Shit, ready to pull up now. Dat nigga better not have us out here fo' no fuckin reasons."

"Naw Hawk. I got trust in brah. I know one thing, he wouldn't risk coming out of hiding just play games wit niggas." Big Dee replied to Hawk's comment.

"Unless dis shit is a hit." Hawk was saying that shit as if he believed the dumb shit he had just uttered.

"Maine shut da fuck up brah." I had to order him. "Back up some so des stinking ass niggas can do whatever dey got to do." As he said they would at the exact time. The garbage men dumped the trash and right before leaving. They filled up two trash cans with two black bags each. "Told you" I had to rub it in Hawk's face. He was speechless. I grabbed one of the trash cans by the handle and started to make my way around the back of the apartment building. Big Dee grab da other one. Hawk go through da front and open da back door for us."

Big Dee and I carted the trash can, we dropped them on the floor of the empty apartment. All three of us ripped hotels into the four bags. In tow of the bags, it was loaded with bricks. It had to be about thirty of them. The other two bags were filled with cash money. It was gone take some time to count all this cash.

Self Made Tay

Chapter 59
Q On the Run

Scene: The crib

"Hello" I had just answered my ringing phone.

"Yo sup Cuz?" It was Top Shotta.

"Supp fool?"

"You know we have a meeting being held today right?"

"Yeah Top Shotta, same place, same time."

"Shiddd. You are usually one of da first ones here Cuz. That's why I called to check up on you. Well, dat and one other reason."

"Wats dat brah?"

"You ight my nigga?" You sound a lil...out of it."

"Yeah, I'm good. Wats up though? You got me hanging on to dis phone a lil too long." I was on the phone and my mind went blank. I heard what he was saying but not really listening. I won't feeling anyone right now. I laid the phone down and picked up the playing card from off the table. It was the Queen of Hearts. I ripped it in half splitting her heart down the middle to make hers feel like mine. Using the corner of one of the half cards, I scooped up a mountain of heroin and snorted it all up into my right nostril. Repeating the process, only this time, I fed the left. Guess the cats are out of the bag now. Looks like I haven't been telling you exactly everything. And so fucking what? Consider it as a factor. Niggas ain't trying to hear the tails of a nigga on his downfall. On top of all of this shit that's happening, I finally found the poison to fill the emptiness of my missing heart.

"Think I'm going to dat fuckin' meeting? Got me fucked up!" Excuse me, I won't talking to anyone but me. Bear with me. "Where da fuck are my keys?" I stood to my feet and staggered over to the kitchen countertop, snatching the keys up. I made my way out the door.

"Mr. Anderson! How are you doing?" I was greeted as I exited the elevator. Fuck, what was that bitch so happy about? I just kept pushing ahead. In my mind, I was concealing my high from the world. Knowing damn well that anybody with eyes could see that I was far from sober.

Scene 2:Stan's House

Twisting the knob to unlock the door, I entered the apartment and made my way upstairs. It was still considered early in the morning for the residents of the projects. It was a few minutes until eight. I wanted to come through and take Stan on a trip before the hood woke up. This nigga was in the bed stretched out underneath the covers. Nudging his shoulder, I attempted to wake him from his sweet dreams. This nigga ait'n budge. Not even a finger. This time shaking him. Ayee brah, get da fuck up fool. We're about to head out. That didn't work either. I pushed him with force. I know dame well this nigga wasn't that much of a heavy sleeper.

I was starting to think Stan's sleep was eternal. I checked his pulse to draw a conclusion. Sad to say, but I guessed right. Although there wasn't a visible wound on Stan's body. I knew he had crossed over to the other side. I tried to cry, but couldn't. It was hard, the drug clouded my mind. The confusion from his death left me stunned. All I knew for sure was that I had to get the fuck out of there. I don't know what's happening but I ain't want to take the blame for it. Please don't judge me on this one. Stan was like a brother to me and I was actually mad at God for taking him. At least, he wasn't in one of the most peaceful ways. Before leaving Stan's crib, I grabbed his cell phone off his nightstand and dialed 911. "Hello. Yes. No. There's a dead body lying in an apartment at da corner of St. James and VV>Hill Street. Huh? Umm…" I just laid the phone on the bed after wiping my prints off. Hopefully, they would be able to track the call or Stan's family would wake up to find him. May God bless them.

I hurried to my Rolls Royce and pulled off slowly. I was already pumping Meek Mill's expensive pain. Ironically, his song "Halo" was up next. I let the words of the song take my soul away as I cruised through the streets of my childhood residence.

"Should I just wear a Halo? Cuz I already know too many angles. I've been riding all my life chasing Dreams? not really paying attention to what it does to my health. And I can tell you this life ain't what it seems. But no matter what it is, I stay true to myself.

I was trying to figure out how I got so fucked up in the head as I pulled up on 2nd Street next to the graveyard. How did I become an accused to death? Why was it that in every place I searched for love, I found the evils of hate? I laid my head on the center of the steering wheel and tried to force a tear from my eyes again. The only cries I had in my head were the calls of angels.

KNOCK, KNOCK, KNOCK I looked up to find Reggie topping on the passenger side window. I plainly hit the button to unlock the doors. "Wats up brah?" Reggie asked joking as he took a seat and closed the door. "You act like you ain't been fuckin' with a nigga. I know' you put niggas on and shit. But you ait'n gotta play big like niggas ain't get it out da mud wit you and shit." He was rambling on, and I let him. "Ayee, I ain't gone like act as though I am a fool. Dat nigga Flex hot as hell; everybody cut his ass off. Now dat nigga pockets getting low again. He's tight as a pussy out here running around like a chicken with his head cut off looking for a plug. Nigga is so thirsty, he begging damn near everybody to let him know what our new connect is. Nigga say dat nigga been putting his face in da work anyway. Breathe all da coke up. I believe it too. He thinks he is saving face. Niggas can't hide dat getting high shit from me. I been seeing dis shit all my life," Reggie paused for a quick second. I was hoping because he was done talking. "Q, what da fuck is wrong wit you brah?" So much for being hopeful. "Why da fuck you ova der actin like a lil bitch? I know you are crying.

"I lifted my head up and looked Reggie dead in his eyes. I'm pretty sure he has never seen this look in my eyes before. Equally so, I've never had this feeling before. I'm not talking about the high. I'm talking about the law. "Brah! I know you ait'n fucking high. Yo ass looks like you're about to die. You need to tighten up brah. We don lost too many niggas and have come too far to fall now. Plus, dis ain't back in da day brah. Niggas making real money out dis bitch. We ain't never been dis lit. I'on know wat you trippin off, but yo' clumsy ass needs to tighten up fool. You are my nigga, and I love you. I ain't trying to see you like dis." I was still staring at Reggie in his eyes. Not even a blink. As he did his version of pouring his heart out. Good to know that he at least still had one to pour from.

"Stan is dead, I broke the ice with the cold news.

"Wat!?" Reggie asked. "Stop playing wit me Q, before I smack da shit out yo ass. I was just with him last night." I shook my head before banging it back on the steering wheel. "How da fuck you know' dis Q? Say some wat da fuck?"

"I just left his house, brah. He must have died in his sleep."

Maine take me 'round der. What da fuck you talking about dying in his sleep? Dat man was young as shit. I need to see for myself. Cuz I'on know' wat stupid shit yo spellin' out yo' mouth"

"Naw brah, it should be round der by now."

"Maine fuck R! Take me to go see my nigga!"

"No!" I had to scream at Reggie, lifting my head up. He looked confused. Like surprised and pissed off at the same damn time. "He good brah. He is good. Da place he going to way better den dis hell. Wish it was me instead."

"Fool yo' ass tripping." Take me to Tiger Mret right quick. I need to get some sandwich bags. And if you eva talk to me like that again, I won't hesitate to smack da shit out you' ass for real."

"Why don't you just go to Wally's? It's round da corner."

"Cuz dey don't ever have shit in dat store. Plus, I wanna see at least if the police pull up at Stan's. For real, police have been scared to come out dis bitch. Dem ma'fuckas don't even respond to crime calls no more."

"Well, you right den. But I'm telling you brah. Do not drive yo' ass down dat hill, especially not in this car."

"Oh shit! Nigga, ready, let a nigga drive da Rolls Royce, say no more, I got you my nigga." I climbed over into the passenger seat and waited for Reggie to travel around the car to take the wheel. That swag was tuned up. I knew the feeling.

Chapter 60
Flex Focus

Scene: St. James Street

"Ight. Yeah, I heard you. Naw I don't know wats dat about." Ayee held up right quick fool. This was Lil Shawty. Let me get this bitch off the phone right quick. I'ma get with you.

"Ight look, I'm a hit you right back cuz I want to handle some shit before you do all dat. Naw, it won't be long at all. And no, it can't wait." I flipped the phone closed and slid it into my pocket. She is talking about a call she just got off from someone reporting a dead body. Say the cover was acting strange and a whole bunch of other shit that I ain't give a damn about.

One thing that I was damned sure about was that damn Rolls Royce that I saw rolling through this bitch again. That little bitch was a hard-headed hoe I see. As promised, I had hit that nigga Gotti Ru up. You remember the nigga from the Exxon? Yeah, I was hoping he had some weight for a nigga. Come to find out, he had something better, and heavier, Guns. Right now I carried an ARP I got from the O.G. The shit was fully stocked with scoop, beam, extra grips, and a shoulder scrap. The last time I saw the Rolls Royce, it was heading up towards 2nd Street, which made sense now that I thought about it. A Lot of traffic has been gravitating up that way lately. Maybe that's where that sneaky bitch was trying to cover up her business.

I loved it when God landed an unplanned murder victim right in a nigga's lap. Coming out of the cut of Saint James block, I spotted the prey I hunted for. At the corner of West Hill and St. James, I upped the ARP and focused in on the dark tinted window. Time to put this bitch in her place. I squeezed on the trigger with no intent of letting up. Bullets flew through the window like jets breaking through clouds. Some rammed through the car door. I took a couple of steps closer thinking I had the bitch defenseless. One thing I was sure to make sure of is that she would not make it out of that car.

Now noticing the passenger side door flying open, I refocused my aim. The bitch wasn't alone. Whoever the nigga was she had with her in that car had balls. He popped out of the car almost on some shit that I would be on blasting two sets of guns in my direction. I could tell they were both Glock 40's. The multitude of shots caused me to duck, trying to find my way back into the cut behind a building. That was until I looked back up to catch the nigga trying to make a run for it. By the time I had the rifle lifted to focus my aim again. He was turning back around and attempted to stretch me again, sending shots like a true gunslinger. Nigga still ain't hit shit. Bullets threaten me. Shooting pass my ear drum, only making music to my ears. It was gone take more than that to get rid of the muscle.

Time to stop playing with this rookie. I continued with my focus and did some rookie shit myself. The only thing that saved me was the fact that the dude was shooting for cover, not a kill. I watched him run around for that split second that my brain froze. I was swearing that this mysterious nigga highly resembled Q. I had a secret to tell you. Yeah nigga, right now! At a time like this, I missed my brother. Just the fact that my mind played these wicked games on me. I desperately wanted to kill this Q imposter. It was too late though. That nigga ran like it was a track meet hopping the gate of the high riser and rounding the corner.

I walked up to the car. Gun up, trying to see if it is clarified that I got the driver. I opened the door only to find Reggie. "Fuck!"

Chapter 61
Q On the Run Part II

I was trying my best to drown out the frivolity of Reggie's words. Then my phone rang. It was Top Shotta. I ignored it twice. Then a text came in. I looked down to read it as Reggie braked at a stop sign.

The text read: //*Wya cuz? Everybody looking for you. Shit not looking good. You have an obligation to be here.* I turned off the scene to my phone leaving it black. The next thing I knew, bullets were rattling the car. Rocking it like the last boat Aalihya was on. Luckily for me, I was already leaning back in the seat, sloped. Unfortunately for Reggie, the shooter was relentless. A quick thought. I know for a fact that a nigga couldn't see Reggie behind these tints, especially considering how black this nigga was, so I figured it wasn't an enemy of his. Someone was aiming to kill the owner of this car. I knew then that it was Flex.

Even after talking about all that, I don't give a fuck shit. I realized that I was still far from stupid. I crawled out of the car ducking as low as possible until I saw an opportunity to send shots at my Opp utilizing booth Glocks on me. It stalled him for a second I needed to get the fuck on. While making a run for my life, my pride kicked in a little. That little was enough for me to make an irrational decision. Why the fuck was I running from this nigga? Aint this the same nigga I wanted to kill? The one that tried to kill me? I turned around to take aim tempting to take the nigga's head off. Then my senses kicked in again as he upped that big-ass gun. I was running for a chance to get back. I had wisely picked and chosen my battles.

I hopped the fence and hauled ass around the corner of the high-rise building. Looks like God still had me in his favor. A GRTC city bus was pulling up to the bus stop right in front of the building. Tucking the hot steel, I climbed on the bus and handed the driver a hundred-dollar bill. That was all I had. Seated in the seat on my way downtown, the image of Reggie covered in blood taking his last breath almost made my lungs collapse. I wondered if Suge felt how I felt at this moment. I know one thing; retaliation was a must.

Chapter 62
Flex Fate
Scene: St. Paul Street

These last few days, I've been feeling tired of myself. Damn near to the point of suicide. To know that Stan and Reggie had lifted their bodies on the same day, within minutes of each other, broke my spine. I know why Reggie was gone. Please don't remind me. If I wasn't so paranoid that niggas were trying to kill me, I swear I would retire my gun. I was killing all the wrong people. For the life of me, I couldn't understand how Stan passed away. At least, for him, it was peaceful, and he had escaped this painful world. Why the fuck did everyone around me get to go and I had to stay? I was starting to get confused about the concept of life. Death was starting to seem like a celebration because the life we lived was nothing to cheer about. Killing each other. Hating each other. For what? What was our real purpose? I know right, why wonder now? It gotta be too late for a nigga like me. I just know when I go, I'm going with a bang. If that's not possible, then I'll look my killer dead in the eyes and tell him thank you. Then spit in his face as a fuck you.

I was thinking about Q every minute of the days that passed. Which was another reason my days and every minute of the days that passed seemed to drag. Strangely, I felt more connected to him, like he was on the other side protecting me from harm, regardless of the pain I brought to him. I sat on some big rocks sticking out of the foundation of the building on the corner of West HIll and St. Paul across the street from Tiger Mart. I sat here with no purpose. Nothing to do. I was out of weight. All I had left was the shit to support my habit. I had money, but no one to share it with or to re-up with. Niggas won't fucking with me. They probably were waiting for me to drop dead from a bursted heart. Since these bitches ain't have the heart to do it, I ain't have anywhere to go either. I wish I could have left with Q back then when he had an escape plan. I fucked my only brother's life up.

My ego told me that was my purpose. He said I was made to fuck shit up. That's exactly what I've done. Hopefully, I was done.

I was so much in my feelings that I didn't even realize the all-black Yukon Denil bending the corner smoothly. I paid no mind to it, even after I Saw it. I should have. Both back doors along with the front passenger popped open and four gunmen jumped out. I knew them all. Two of them grabbed me by the arms and threw me in the car. "Jay Jr!" I was lost. "Where da fuck you come from?" I had to ask as the rest jumped back in the car. That little nigga went upside my head with the butt of the pistol.

"Shut da fuck up nigga! Ain't nobody asked you to talk.!" I felt blood leaking from the split on my head immediately flowing down my face. Looking around the car, it was Big Dee, Hawk, Blu, Red, and even Wolf.

"Wolf?" I disregarded Jay Jr's order. "Come on Lil brah. You gone back door a nigga like dat?" I was helpless.

"I learned from da best." Wolf just shrugged his shoulders. My disrespect earned me another crack on the head. "If you don't shut da fuck up, yo ass gone die before you go to meet ya maker."

"Come on y'all, don't kill me, let somebody else do it. Not y'all, please." Crack, crack. I was growing dizzy now.

"Oh, we are gonna let somebody else kill you. You lucky I'on do it," Hawk said from the front seat. "If it was up to me, I'd stab your ass every hour. 24 hours, 24 stabs. Make yo' ass take a whole day to die or bleed out. Whichever came first." My mind was scrambling trying to figure out who the fuck they were taking me to and where.

Being that the drive was so short, I soon found out the location of my destination. The truck drove through the open gates of the graveyard on 2nd Street. I'm pretty sure you know the story of this place. We were all here once before. The truck parked face to face with another car. The gang that used to be my gang, yanked me out of the car. They walked me over to the other vehicle. The back door of the car opened and would you believe it? I almost fainted. You probably knew the whole time. I thought this nigga was dead.

I thought I had surely finished him. The phone in my pocket started to ring.

Chapter 63
Q's Quietus

Scene: Graveyard

"Wat's wrong Flex? You look like you just saw a ghost?" A nefarious smirk stretched across my face. That statement could never get too old in my book. The nigga damn near passed out at the sight of me; pretty sure it was the worst thing that he could ever imagine like the devil destined to battle the opposite version of himself. "Damn lil big bra. You don't seem to be happy to see me. What, you don't miss a nigga? Not even a lil?" Big Dee and Hawk were holding Flex up barely by both arms. "Yall can let da nigga go. He ain't going nowhere but to the ground." They did just that allowing Flex's pre-lifeless body to tumble to the ground.

There was a phone in Flex's pocket that was ringing off the hook, sort of say, "somebody get dat fuckin' phone off him please?" Hawk was the one to rip the phone out of Flex's pocket. He tossed the flip to me. I caught it and slid it into my own pocket for now. "Ayee Wolf, go grab da shovels. I want you to help dis nigga dig his own grave out. Gotta make sure you're really down, feel me?" Wolf simply nodded his head in agreement as he walked past me to grab the shelves out of the trunk of the car I had just gotten out of. Before he could get out of arm's reach, I gripped the upper part of his arm with condensed pressure. I pulled the lil nigga in a bit closer and hinted into his ear. Making myself clear as I spoke. "Trust me on dis promise young nigga, if you do anything in an attempt to save dis piece of shit ass nigga, I'ma make dem niggas bury yo' ass in da same hole as dat dead bastard. You understand?"

"Now...I mean yeah. I got you Q" The little nigga was definitely nervous. A good soldier. Just misguided. "I'm just tryna do wat I got to do brah."

"Good man. You are smart. Now go handle your business." By the time Wolf was returning with the two shovels, Flex's phone was erupting with another set of rings. Shit was getting on my last fucking nerves. Whoever it was must have wanted something very important. I wondered who wanted to talk to this scum bag so fucking bad. "Let me see dat." I snatched one of the shelves from Wolf as he moved to settle back in his place. Taking the phone outta my pocket, I dropped it to the ground of the grass. I could care less who was trying to reach him. "I hope you said your goodbyes to whoever da fuck dis is." I used the tip of the shovel head and stabbed the phone multiple times until it was smashed into pieces.

"Now," I said, walking over to Flex, throwing the shovel to the ground in front of him. His knees in the dirt were the only thing that kept him upright. "Let's get to business." Another interruption. It was another ringing phone. That's when I realized I had broken my own rule by bringing my phone along with me on a kill. I was trying to keep my words intact with so many other letters that I forgot to dot my I's. I looked at the name of the caller coming in on the face of my phone. It was supreme. I thought about answering but said fuck it. Little did he know that I planned to pay him a visit right after I was down here. I won't run from shit from now on. Running is what got me in this shit in the first place. Plus, I no longer had to answer to no one. Not a soul. Per me, I turned the phone off and slid it back into my pocket for now.

"Come on man, get yo ass up," I demanded Flex. "Grab a shovel, get to digging. Wolf! Help him." To my surprise, Flex actually used his muscle to dig his own resting place, making himself his own grave digger. I couldn't find a drop of sympathy for the nigga. Something that I learned about life was that we all got exactly what we deserve. Whether good or bad, it was all on you. It's best to be careful how you make your bed. Because soon, you would surely have to lie in it, or in Flex's case, grave. "Yall niggas hurry da fuck up! We got other shit to do." They were already at the halfway mark by this point. I pulled out one of my Glock 40s preparing to taste the sweetness of revenge.

I was astonished when two all-black Cadillac Escalades turned into the graveyard with supreme confidence. Everyone with me stood by my side except Flex. He stood watching with the shovel he still had in hand. It made perfectly good sense moments later when Supreme stepped out the back of the second truck. He was surrounded by two guards who traveled with him in my direction. Four more guys stood back with assault rifles in their hands. Two a piece for each truck. Split on both sides.

"Jeremiah 13." He was holding both of his hands halfway up with the same smirk I had on my face not too long ago as if he was happy to see me. "My long lost child. One of my favorites by the way. I've found you again. This is truly a blessing. Did you think you could just run off and go free like this? You've abandoned us, my child. Did you not think that I wouldn't have an eye on your every move." I looked around at everyone around me. I knew not to trust a soul at this stage of my life. Them niggas were looking back at me as if they were ready for the word to kill.

"Who da fuck is Jeremiah 13?" Hawk asked, always looking for the right answers. "Q who da fuck is dis nigga? And how many names do you have? Who da fuck are you?"

I looked over to Hawk and Shook my head as lightly as I could. Shifting my eyes to Big Dee, we made contact. From there, all I could do was hope that he would be read right. My right hand went up as fast as possible while the left was whipping my other gun from under my belt. Before I could even lift the second gun, two bullets were exiting the first one. They both slammed into the body of the big bodyguard causing him to hit the ground hard. Thankfully, the team is on point. I aimed my second gun at the second bodyguard causing them to hit the ground hard. He was moving fast. One of my members had aimed for Supreme. The bodyguard jumped in front of the bullets and sacrificed himself for his so-called master. Talking about taking your job too seriously.

To my surprise, Supreme had pulled out a gun of his own. It was a P90. Wisely though, he backed peddled, shadowing himself into the crowd of shit as he fired shots towards us. We all scattered in our own directions hiding behind tombstones, cars, or whatever shield we could use. There were many bullets raining, like the spring season bringing life to the earth. However, this rain poured in seeking to cause death. I made my way to the back of my DTS to find Flex ducking behind the truck. He was startled when he saw me raise the gun to his face. "Brah, think!" He raised his hands up in defense. "I can help you."

"Help me!? Nigga you already helped me enough don't you think? I should smoke up your snake ass right now. But I at least respect you enough to bury yo' ass first"

"Q! Please miss me with all dat bullshit. And give me a fuckin gun. When we make it out dis shit we could handle it however you want to."

I couldn't believe that I was actually considering this nigga's suggestion. It only made sense if I knew that I would be able to trust the nigga. The past events of my life would prove that I couldn't do that. It seemed like from out of nowhere, sirens were blasting brazen sounds that were probably about to pull up on us like right...Now "Fuck!" I cursed myself out loud. Where the fuck did they come from after all this time? Now, all of a sudden, they want to pull up. And since when did they ever pull up during shooting? Where the fuck do they do that at? I had two of them, but went against my better judgment and popped the trunk of the car. Inside it were two Draco's. I put my Glocks back on my waist and grabbed one Draco handing it to Flex. I took the other one for myself.

Flex held the Draco as if he was making love to it. "Now dat's wat da fuck I'm talking about." The crazy bitch kissed the gun. To keep it real brah, you almost had me fooled. But now I'm convinced. Some shit never changes. You may never learn. Intelligence over emotion."

"Maine shut da fuck up and go do wat you do best."

"After you stupid."

"Together," we both said in unison. I flipped to the left around the right side of the car, gun up. Flex ran around the other side creeping low. Together, we stood tall banging bullets out of the Drac's back-to-back. It was more police than I thought. They weren't too much of a problem though. Flex was dropping them like roaches getting touched by raid. I took most of my aim at the niggas supreme brought to tag along to this death festival. I got rid of quite a few of them. Just couldn't get Supreme. I couldn't leave here without killing him, or I'll forever be hunted. I scanned the graveyard to make sure that all my niggas were good. I just had that feeling. Sure enough, as soon as I did, my eyes were cursed again having to see Jay Jr. being riddled with too many bullets to count.

Big Dee screamed out in agonizing pain. We all went crazy shooting relentlessly. Back to back; the opps were dropping. They were so stupid they were even killing each other. Police killing society members and vice versa. While we helped kill them all. Flex did something that instantly earned my appreciation. Not sure how he did it. He was able to get the perfect aim on Supreme. He used the bullets of the Draco to rip the man's body into pieces like a sheet of paper. The remaining members of Supreme camp were loading up their vehicle in an attempt to make a get-away. I wasn't too fond of letting that happen.

I called myself chasing down the car piercing the metal with bullets, creating more holes that were already there. They were making a run for it, still not giving up on the shooting though. Damn, nearly every passenger of the car sent shots out the window. They won't let up and neither was I. What the fuck was I thinking though? The next thing I knew, I was thinking nothing. Two bullets entered my brain. The second definitely ended me. I was finished flat-lined.

The End of Life As I Know It...

To Be Continued...
Born in the Grave 3
Coming Soon

Lock Down Publications and Ca$h Presents assisted publishing packages.

BASIC PACKAGE $499
Editing
Cover Design
Formatting

UPGRADED PACKAGE $800
Typing
Editing
Cover Design
Formatting

ADVANCE PACKAGE $1,200
Typing
Editing
Cover Design
Formatting
Copyright registration
Proofreading
Upload book to Amazon

LDP SUPREME PACKAGE $1,500
Typing
Editing
Cover Design
Formatting
Copyright registration
Proofreading
Set up Amazon account
Upload book to Amazon
Advertise on LDP Amazon and Facebook page

***Other services available upon request. Additional charges may apply
Lock Down Publications
P.O. Box 944

Stockbridge, GA 30281-9998
Phone # 470 303-9761

Submission Guideline

Submit the first three chapters of your completed manuscript to ldpsubmissions@gmail.com, subject line: Your book's title. The manuscript must be in a .doc file and sent as an attachment. Document should be in Times New Roman, double spaced and in size 12 font. Also, provide your synopsis and full contact information. If sending multiple submissions, they must each be in a separate email.

Have a story but no way to send it electronically? You can still submit to LDP/Ca$h Presents. Send in the first three chapters, written or typed, of your completed manuscript to:

LDP: Submissions Dept
Po Box 944
Stockbridge, Ga 30281

DO NOT send original manuscript. Must be a duplicate.

Provide your synopsis and a cover letter containing your full contact information.

Thanks for considering LDP and Ca$h Presents.

NEW RELEASES

CRIME BOSS by PLAYA RAY

LOYALTY IS EVERYTHING by MOLOTTI

HERE TODAY GONE TOMORROW by FLY ROCK

A GANGSTA'S KARMA 3 by FLAME

BORN IN THE GRAVE 2 by SELF MADE TAY

STRAIGHT BEAST MODE III

De'Kari

KINGPIN KILLAZ IV

STREET KINGS III

PAID IN BLOOD III

CARTEL KILLAZ IV

DOPE GODS III

Hood Rich

SINS OF A HUSTLA II

ASAD

YAYO V

Bred In The Game 2

S. Allen

THE STREETS WILL TALK II

By Yolanda Moore

SON OF A DOPE FIEND III

HEAVEN GOT A GHETTO II

SKI MASK MONEY II

By Renta

LOYALTY AIN'T PROMISED III

By Keith Williams

I'M NOTHING WITHOUT HIS LOVE II

SINS OF A THUG II

TO THE THUG I LOVED BEFORE II

IN A HUSTLER I TRUST II

By Monet Dragun

QUIET MONEY IV

EXTENDED CLIP III

THUG LIFE IV

By **Trai'Quan**

THE STREETS MADE ME IV

By **Larry D. Wright**

IF YOU CROSS ME ONCE II

ANGEL V

By **Anthony Fields**

THE STREETS WILL NEVER CLOSE IV

By **K'ajji**

HARD AND RUTHLESS III

KILLA KOUNTY IV

By **Khufu**

MONEY GAME III

By **Smoove Dolla**

JACK BOYS VS DOPE BOYS IV

A GANGSTA'S QUR'AN V

COKE GIRLZ II

COKE BOYS II

LIFE OF A SAVAGE V

CHI'RAQ GANGSTAS V

By **Romell Tukes**

MURDA WAS THE CASE III

Elijah R. Freeman

THE STREETS NEVER LET GO III

By **Robert Baptiste**

AN UNFORESEEN LOVE IV

BABY, I'M WINTERTIME COLD II

By **Meesha**

MONEY MAFIA II

By **Jibril Williams**

QUEEN OF THE ZOO III

By **Black Migo**
VICIOUS LOYALTY III
By Kingpen
A GANGSTA'S PAIN III
By J-Blunt
CONFESSIONS OF A JACKBOY III
By Nicholas Lock
GRIMEY WAYS III
By Ray Vinci
KING KILLA II
By Vincent "Vitto" Holloway
BETRAYAL OF A THUG III
By Fre$h
THE MURDER QUEENS III
By Michael Gallon
THE BIRTH OF A GANGSTER III
By Delmont Player
TREAL LOVE II
By Le'Monica Jackson
FOR THE LOVE OF BLOOD III
By Jamel Mitchell
RAN OFF ON DA PLUG II
By Paper Boi Rari
HOOD CONSIGLIERE III
By Keese
PRETTY GIRLS DO NASTY THINGS II
By Nicole Goosby
PROTÉGÉ OF A LEGEND II
By Corey Robinson
IT'S JUST ME AND YOU II

Self Made Tay

By Ah'Million
BORN IN THE GRAVE III
By Self Made Tay
FOREVER GANGSTA III
By Adrian Dulan
GORILLAZ IN THE TRENCHES II
By SayNoMore
THE COCAINE PRINCESS VI
By King Rio
CRIME BOSS II
Playa Ray
LOYALTY IS EVERYTHING II
Molotti
HERE TODAY GONE TOMORROW II
By Fly Rock

Available Now

RESTRAINING ORDER **I & II**
By **CA$H & Coffee**
LOVE KNOWS NO BOUNDARIES **I II & III**
By **Coffee**
RAISED AS A GOON I, II, III & IV
BRED BY THE SLUMS I, II, III
BLAST FOR ME I & II
ROTTEN TO THE CORE I II III
A BRONX TALE I, II, III

DUFFLE BAG CARTEL I II III IV V VI

HEARTLESS GOON I II III IV V

A SAVAGE DOPEBOY I II

DRUG LORDS I II III

CUTTHROAT MAFIA I II

KING OF THE TRENCHES

By **Ghost**

LAY IT DOWN **I & II**

LAST OF A DYING BREED I II

BLOOD STAINS OF A SHOTTA I & II III

By **Jamaica**

LOYAL TO THE GAME I II III

LIFE OF SIN I, II III

By **TJ & Jelissa**

BLOODY COMMAS I & II

SKI MASK CARTEL I II & III

KING OF NEW YORK I II,III IV V

RISE TO POWER I II III

COKE KINGS I II III IV V

BORN HEARTLESS I II III IV

KING OF THE TRAP I II

By **T.J. Edwards**

IF LOVING HIM IS WRONG...I & II

LOVE ME EVEN WHEN IT HURTS I II III

By **Jelissa**

WHEN THE STREETS CLAP BACK I & II III

THE HEART OF A SAVAGE I II III IV

MONEY MAFIA

LOYAL TO THE SOIL I II III

By **Jibril Williams**

A DISTINGUISHED THUG STOLE MY HEART I II & III

LOVE SHOULDN'T HURT I II III IV

RENEGADE BOYS I II III IV

PAID IN KARMA I II III

SAVAGE STORMS I II III

AN UNFORESEEN LOVE I II III

BABY, I'M WINTERTIME COLD

By **Meesha**

A GANGSTER'S CODE I &, II III

A GANGSTER'S SYN I II III

THE SAVAGE LIFE I II III

CHAINED TO THE STREETS I II III

BLOOD ON THE MONEY I II III

A GANGSTA'S PAIN I II

By J-Blunt

PUSH IT TO THE LIMIT

By **Bre' Hayes**

BLOOD OF A BOSS **I, II, III, IV, V**

SHADOWS OF THE GAME

TRAP BASTARD

By **Askari**

THE STREETS BLEED MURDER **I, II & III**

THE HEART OF A GANGSTA I II& III

By **Jerry Jackson**

CUM FOR ME I II III IV V VI VII VIII

An **LDP Erotica Collaboration**

BRIDE OF A HUSTLA **I II & II**

THE FETTI GIRLS **I, II& III**

CORRUPTED BY A GANGSTA I, II III, IV

BLINDED BY HIS LOVE

THE PRICE YOU PAY FOR LOVE I, II ,III

DOPE GIRL MAGIC I II III

By **Destiny Skai**

WHEN A GOOD GIRL GOES BAD

By **Adrienne**

THE COST OF LOYALTY I II III

By Kweli

A GANGSTER'S REVENGE **I II III & IV**

THE BOSS MAN'S DAUGHTERS I II III IV V

A SAVAGE LOVE **I & II**

BAE BELONGS TO ME I II

A HUSTLER'S DECEIT I, II, III

WHAT BAD BITCHES DO I, II, III

SOUL OF A MONSTER I II III

KILL ZONE

A DOPE BOY'S QUEEN I II III

TIL DEATH

By **Aryanna**

A KINGPIN'S AMBITON

A KINGPIN'S AMBITION **II**

I MURDER FOR THE DOUGH

By **Ambitious**

TRUE SAVAGE I II III IV V VI VII

DOPE BOY MAGIC I, II, III

MIDNIGHT CARTEL I II III

CITY OF KINGZ I II

NIGHTMARE ON SILENT AVE

THE PLUG OF LIL MEXICO II

CLASSIC CITY

By **Chris Green**

A DOPEBOY'S PRAYER

By **Eddie "Wolf" Lee**

THE KING CARTEL **I, II & III**

By **Frank Gresham**

THESE NIGGAS AIN'T LOYAL **I, II & III**

By **Nikki Tee**

GANGSTA SHYT **I II &III**

By **CATO**

THE ULTIMATE BETRAYAL

By **Phoenix**

BOSS'N UP **I , II & III**

By **Royal Nicole**

I LOVE YOU TO DEATH

By **Destiny J**

I RIDE FOR MY HITTA

I STILL RIDE FOR MY HITTA

By **Misty Holt**

LOVE & CHASIN' PAPER

By **Qay Crockett**

TO DIE IN VAIN

SINS OF A HUSTLA

By **ASAD**

BROOKLYN HUSTLAZ

By **Boogsy Morina**

BROOKLYN ON LOCK I & II

By **Sonovia**

GANGSTA CITY

By **Teddy Duke**

A DRUG KING AND HIS DIAMOND I & II III

A DOPEMAN'S RICHES

HER MAN, MINE'S TOO I, II

CASH MONEY HO'S

THE WIFEY I USED TO BE I II

PRETTY GIRLS DO NASTY THINGS

By Nicole Goosby

TRAPHOUSE KING **I II & III**

KINGPIN KILLAZ I II III

STREET KINGS I II

PAID IN BLOOD **I II**

CARTEL KILLAZ I II III

DOPE GODS I II

By **Hood Rich**

LIPSTICK KILLAH **I, II, III**

CRIME OF PASSION I II & III

FRIEND OR FOE I II III

By **Mimi**

STEADY MOBBN' **I, II, III**

THE STREETS STAINED MY SOUL I II III

By **Marcellus Allen**

WHO SHOT YA **I, II, III**

SON OF A DOPE FIEND I II

HEAVEN GOT A GHETTO

SKI MASK MONEY

Renta

GORILLAZ IN THE BAY **I II III IV**

TEARS OF A GANGSTA I II

3X KRAZY I II

STRAIGHT BEAST MODE I II

DE'KARI

TRIGGADALE I II III

MURDAROBER WAS THE CASE I II

Elijah R. Freeman

GOD BLESS THE TRAPPERS I, II, III

THESE SCANDALOUS STREETS I, II, III

FEAR MY GANGSTA I, II, III IV, V

THESE STREETS DON'T LOVE NOBODY I, II

BURY ME A G I, II, III, IV, V

A GANGSTA'S EMPIRE I, II, III, IV

THE DOPEMAN'S BODYGAURD I II

THE REALEST KILLAZ I II III

THE LAST OF THE OGS I II III

Tranay Adams

THE STREETS ARE CALLING

Duquie Wilson

MARRIED TO A BOSS I II III

By Destiny Skai & Chris Green

KINGZ OF THE GAME I II III IV V VI

CRIME BOSS

Playa Ray

SLAUGHTER GANG I II III

RUTHLESS HEART I II III

By Willie Slaughter

FUK SHYT

By Blakk Diamond

DON'T F#CK WITH MY HEART I II

By Linnea

ADDICTED TO THE DRAMA I II III

IN THE ARM OF HIS BOSS II

By Jamila

YAYO I II III IV

A SHOOTER'S AMBITION I II

BRED IN THE GAME

By S. Allen

TRAP GOD I II III

RICH $AVAGE I II III

MONEY IN THE GRAVE I II III

By Martell Troublesome Bolden

FOREVER GANGSTA I II

GLOCKS ON SATIN SHEETS I II

By Adrian Dulan

TOE TAGZ I II III IV

LEVELS TO THIS SHYT I II

IT'S JUST ME AND YOU

By Ah'Million

KINGPIN DREAMS I II III

RAN OFF ON DA PLUG

By Paper Boi Rari

CONFESSIONS OF A GANGSTA I II III IV

CONFESSIONS OF A JACKBOY I II

By Nicholas Lock

I'M NOTHING WITHOUT HIS LOVE

SINS OF A THUG

TO THE THUG I LOVED BEFORE

A GANGSTA SAVED XMAS

IN A HUSTLER I TRUST

By Monet Dragun

CAUGHT UP IN THE LIFE I II III

THE STREETS NEVER LET GO I II

By Robert Baptiste

NEW TO THE GAME I II III

MONEY, MURDER & MEMORIES I II III
By **Malik D. Rice**
LIFE OF A SAVAGE I II III IV
A GANGSTA'S QUR'AN I II III IV
MURDA SEASON I II III
GANGLAND CARTEL I II III
CHI'RAQ GANGSTAS I II III IV
KILLERS ON ELM STREET I II III
JACK BOYZ N DA BRONX I II III
A DOPEBOY'S DREAM I II III
JACK BOYS VS DOPE BOYS I II III
COKE GIRLZ
COKE BOYS
By Romell Tukes
LOYALTY AIN'T PROMISED I II
By Keith Williams
QUIET MONEY I II III
THUG LIFE I II III
EXTENDED CLIP I II
A GANGSTA'S PARADISE
By **Trai'Quan**
THE STREETS MADE ME I II III
By **Larry D. Wright**
THE ULTIMATE SACRIFICE I, II, III, IV, V, VI
KHADIFI
IF YOU CROSS ME ONCE
ANGEL I II III IV
IN THE BLINK OF AN EYE
By **Anthony Fields**
THE LIFE OF A HOOD STAR

By Ca$h & Rashia Wilson
THE STREETS WILL NEVER CLOSE I II III
By K'ajji
CREAM I II III
THE STREETS WILL TALK
By Yolanda Moore
NIGHTMARES OF A HUSTLA I II III
By King Dream
CONCRETE KILLA I II III
VICIOUS LOYALTY I II
By Kingpen
HARD AND RUTHLESS I II
MOB TOWN 251
THE BILLIONAIRE BENTLEYS I II III
By Von Diesel
GHOST MOB
Stilloan Robinson
MOB TIES I II III IV V VI
SOUL OF A HUSTLER, HEART OF A KILLER
GORILLAZ IN THE TRENCHES
By SayNoMore
BODYMORE MURDERLAND I II III
THE BIRTH OF A GANGSTER I II
By Delmont Player
FOR THE LOVE OF A BOSS
By C. D. Blue
MOBBED UP I II III IV
THE BRICK MAN I II III IV
THE COCAINE PRINCESS I II III IV V
By King Rio

KILLA KOUNTY I II III IV
By Khufu
MONEY GAME I II
By Smoove Dolla
A GANGSTA'S KARMA I II III
By FLAME
KING OF THE TRENCHES I II III
by **GHOST & TRANAY ADAMS**
QUEEN OF THE ZOO I II
By **Black Migo**
GRIMEY WAYS I II
By Ray Vinci
XMAS WITH AN ATL SHOOTER
By Ca$h & Destiny Skai
KING KILLA
By Vincent "Vitto" Holloway
BETRAYAL OF A THUG I II
By Fre$h
THE MURDER QUEENS I II
By Michael Gallon
TREAL LOVE
By Le'Monica Jackson
FOR THE LOVE OF BLOOD I II
By Jamel Mitchell
HOOD CONSIGLIERE I II
By Keese
PROTÉGÉ OF A LEGEND
By Corey Robinson
BORN IN THE GRAVE I II
By Self Made Tay

MOAN IN MY MOUTH

By XTASY

TORN BETWEEN A GANGSTER AND A GENTLEMAN

By J-BLUNT & Miss Kim

LOYALTY IS EVERYTHING

Molotti

HERE TODAY GONE TOMORROW

By Fly Rock

<u>BOOKS BY LDP'S CEO, CA$H</u>

TRUST IN NO MAN

TRUST IN NO MAN 2

TRUST IN NO MAN 3

BONDED BY BLOOD

SHORTY GOT A THUG

THUGS CRY

THUGS CRY 2

THUGS CRY 3

TRUST NO BITCH

TRUST NO BITCH 2

TRUST NO BITCH 3

TIL MY CASKET DROPS

RESTRAINING ORDER

RESTRAINING ORDER 2

IN LOVE WITH A CONVICT

LIFE OF A HOOD STAR

XMAS WITH AN ATL SHOOTER

Born in the Grave 2